First published in Canada by Tradewind Books in 2010
Released in the US in 2011

LIBRARY AND ARCHIVES CANADA CATALOGUING IN PUBLICATION
Superle, Michelle
    Black dog dream dog / Michelle Superle ; illustrated
by Millie Ballance.

ISBN 978-1-896580-34-0

    I. Ballance, Millie II. Title.

PS8637.U65B53 2010   jC813'.6   C2010-902918-6

CATALOGUING-IN-PUBLICATION DATA AVAILABLE FROM THE BRITISH LIBRARY.

Book & cover design by Elisa Gutiérrez

Printed in Canada on 100% ancient
forest friendly paper.
2 4 6 8 10 9 7 5 3 1

Manufactured in Canada by Sunrise Printing
Chilliwack, BC November 2010

FSC
Mixed Sources
Cert no. SW-COC-001271
© 1996 FSC

The publisher thanks the Canada Council for the Arts for its support. The publisher also wishes to thank the Government of British Columbia for the financial support it has extended through the book publishing tax credit program and the British Columbia Arts Council. The publisher also aknowledges the financial support of the Government of Canada through the Canada Book Fund and the Livres Canada Books.

Canada Council   Conseil des Arts
for the Arts   du Canada

BRITISH
COLUMBIA
ARTS COUNCIL.

Michelle Superle

BLACK DOG
Dream DOG

illustrated by Millie Ballance

Vancouver · London

For the real Horatio, who was a dream come true, and for all the lost, lonely dogs who need a loving home. —MS

• • •

Many thanks to Alison Acheson, a patient and talented writing teacher, and also to Kim Aippersbach for her fine, tireless editorial guidance.

For Nutty and Angus—MB

Contents

The dog waited in the backyard for her until it was dark. He was anxious and hungry. She was never this late—where was she? He could smell other people's dinners, the delicious food smells wafting out from the surrounding houses. Chicken next door. Salmon across the street. Steak barbequing a few houses down. A thin icicle of drool escaped his mouth. He sighed and put his chin on his paws.

He spent the whole night outside, something he'd never done before. It was scary sometimes with the shadows shifting and the bushes rustling. He'd been brave and stopped himself from howling, because that's the kind of dog he was. In the morning, he heard the neighbours leaving for work, car doors and front doors slamming one after another. Soon the street was quiet with morning stillness. And she hadn't returned yet.

He nosed at the back door, hoping it would open. He peeked into the house through a low window, but nothing had changed since yesterday morning. He barked, once, but nobody came.

The dog was very worried now. He had to find her. He trotted through the yard and slipped through the loose fence boards into the woods. He wandered all day, though he didn't find her. But he wouldn't give up.

Chapter 1

SAM

As soon as Sam Hudson walked through the door to her house, she knew her favourite meal was cooking for dinner. Of course. It was Tuesday—stew day. Sam loved chicken stew, but she clenched her fists. If only something exciting would happen. Something different. Something she couldn't predict by the day of the week. Something that would make her life—*her*—less boring.

It drove Sam crazy, the way her mom organized every corner of her life. Sam was only allowed to choose the clothes she wanted to wear and which books she would read. And *nothing* she said to her mom made her listen. "Don't worry about making decisions. You're only eleven. Leave that to me—it's my job." It made Sam feel like there was an iron band clamped around her throat.

While Sam stood there inhaling the damp smells of chicken, carrots and celery, Mom materialized from upstairs. Sam's small delight in the salty stew smells trickled away. Even when Piglet, her West Highland terrier, launched himself at Sam and quivered with happiness that she was home, Sam felt her throat close.

"Hi, sweetie! What did you learn today?" asked Mom, as she did every afternoon.

Sam dreaded this moment. If her answer wasn't thoughtful enough, Mom's forehead creased and her lips tightened, creating a snaky knot that twisted in Sam's stomach.

Sam liked learning stuff at school, but she didn't like *talking* about it. Talking about it made her feel all itchy, like ants were running up and down her legs. But Mom wouldn't leave her alone until Sam came up with a good answer. She smoothed her hands along Piglet's silky back, thinking.

"Well...we took a nature walk in the woods and learned about how the plants and animals and bugs all work together."

"Excellent!" Mom clapped her hands. "The inter-connectedness of an ecosystem relevant to our own bioecoclimatic zone!"

Sam sighed. Mom was always like this. It was just a nature walk. Sam didn't say that she had really been looking around the woods for spiderwebs covered with dewdrops.

"Come on, Sam, snack time for you. We've got to feed your brain!" said Mom.

Sam sat at the kitchen table, munching her way through crunchy apple slices spread with almond butter. She wished they were cookies and Kool-Aid, but that would never happen because Mom only believed in healthy food. As usual, Piglet waited for the bits Sam didn't want. His little paws bounced up lightly onto her legs. He made her smile, and then her smile widened.

One hour. She had one hour to do whatever she wanted. It was Tuesday, which meant that after school she'd gone to her hour-long computer tutoring session at Mr. Fremont's house. Soccer practice was later that night. Mondays were piano lessons, Wednesdays and Fridays were Tae Kwon Do and Thursdays were Girl Guides. On Saturday mornings Sam had swimming lessons and on Sundays there were soccer games, which she hated. Plus, after dinner there was forty minutes of homework per night, and twenty minutes of either piano or Tae Kwon Do practice. Mom wanted Sam to be well-rounded, whatever that was supposed to mean.

But here was a sliver of time stolen from her schedule. Sam could almost feel the soft deep couch in the living room, Piglet tucked up against her. Soon would come the sweet slipping feeling of disappearing into a book's world. Right now she was reading *Anne of Avonlea*. She melted right inside Anne's adventures—adventures that could *never* happen in her own world, especially not with her mom watching and hovering and organizing everything.

But Mom had other plans.

"Sam, you need to clean your room," she said firmly. When Mom used that tone of voice it was useless to argue with her. Actually, thought Sam, it was *always* useless to argue with her. She tried anyway.

"But Mom! I'm so tired. I just want to hang out on the couch for a while."

"No, Sam. Your room is a mess. Up you go. I'll check it before dinner."

Sam filled up with crackling energy. Bolts of lightening should shoot out of her eyes, she thought. Then she could set her mom's shoes on fire so her mom would have to dance away, like a witch in a fairy tale.

When she got to her room, Sam slammed the door and leaned against it. Her room wasn't *that* messy. What would happen if she didn't tidy it? She scanned the clothes on the floor and the toys in the corner. Her book was here! She could read after all.

Sam opened the book. She waited for the world to melt away. Usually the creaking of the house, the faint distant hissing of traffic on the street outside, the rustling of the trees, all disappeared in seconds. Today, nothing. Sam sighed. She was too restless. Piglet nuzzled, looking for pats. But still the iron band squeezed Sam's throat.

Then a movement in the window caught the corner of her eye. Sam threw down the book, startling Piglet into a yap, and walked over to the window.

Something big and black was standing in her backyard, looking up at her. It was standing in the middle of the grass, in the wild backyard, all alone. Wagging its tail. Where had it come from? Forest tumbled down into the yard, with thick bunches of ferns, salal and blackberry bushes that bears sometimes snacked on. Was it a bear? Sam felt her heart beat faster with excitement.

Chapter 2

SAM

SAM STARED AT THE BLACK CREATURE. This wasn't a bear. It was a huge dog.

The dog stared up at Sam steadily and insistently. She tried smiling at it. The dog wagged its tail in response. But that was crazy—there was no way it could see her up here.

Sam made a decision in a heartbeat and deposited Piglet on her bed. She couldn't shimmy down the rope ladder with him, and anyway, he would be a menace with a new big dog in the yard. He'd just yap his silly head off. Sam needed to be stealthy.

Sam pulled her fire-escape rope ladder out from under her bed. It would only be the third time she'd used it: the other times were during a Hudson family practice fire drill, and a few weeks ago when she'd sneaked outside. Maybe to run away. She'd chickened out that time though.

This time was different. As soon as Sam's feet touched the ground, the dog was there. Its tail wagged so hard she thought it might fly right off its body. Sam crouched down. "Good dog, come here, good dog."

The dog seemed to be smiling. Still wagging, it gently sniffed Sam's hands and face. Sam looked sideways at it and lifted her hand to the dog's head. It nuzzled into Sam and butted its head up into her hand. She patted and stroked, patted and stroked.

Sam finally stood up to take a good look at the dog. It was male and had long black hair and brown eyes. He looked like a loveable golden retriever, except black and twice as big, which was *big*. His head rested on Sam's shoulder.

The longer she stood there patting him, his breath steaming over her cheek, the more a feeling of peace flowed through her. The dog radiated an air of happy calm. Sam's earlier feelings of restlessness drained away. The muscles around her throat unclenched so that the horrible tightness eased and melted. They stood there for what seemed like ages. Sam wanted the good feeling to last forever.

Maybe the dog could be hers. Her new amazing dog. *That* would be exciting. She knew she should tell her mom. But Mom would only send the dog to the pound. Maybe somebody else loved the dog and missed him terribly? *No.* Sam shoved down the thought.

The dog was filthy. Sam's hands were covered with black muck. There was mud dried onto the dog's long feathery tail fur, and his whole coat, which should have been silky and shiny, was tangled, dull and sticky.

It was the filth that gave Sam the clue. This dog was lost! He had nobody to take care of him. Her heart pounded faster. *She* could help him. The thought filled her with a strange hopeful feeling. It would be an adventure to rescue a big mysterious dog.

"What happened to you? Somebody must have really hurt you. You poor thing! You must be hungry. Would you like to stay here?" she asked him.

His ears rose up and tilted forward like sails. His whole body wagged.

Sam's stomach flipped. She could do this. But Mom could never find out. She would be in *huge* trouble if she got caught. And what if somebody *was* missing him? It was really bad to sneak around behind your parents' backs. But still...the dog was so...right.

The thing she had always wished for was happening. For the first time in her eleven years, something exciting had finally trotted into her boring life.

. . .

STELLA

Stella Sylvan woke slowly, slowly, like she was crawling out of a black pit. She opened her eyes and looked around. White walls, blue curtains, green trees, brown dresser and lamp. She blinked. These were not *her* walls, *her* curtains, *her* trees, *her* dresser and lamp. Stella's heart began to pound and she struggled to sit up. It pounded harder when she realized she couldn't.

Where am I? How did I get here? Why am I here?

She tried to call out, to shout the questions, but she couldn't do that either.

"You're awake!" A nurse walked into the white-walled room.

Stella looked at her, the pounding of her heart filling her ears and a hundred questions crowding her mind.

"Oh dear, you must be surprised to find yourself here. Let me explain what's happening."

Stella breathed.

"First, let me introduce myself. I'm Nurse Green. Pleased to meet you, Mrs. Sylvan." She reached across and picked up Stella's limp right hand in hers. "You're at Birchwood Retirement Home, Mrs. Sylvan. You had a stroke about a week ago, and you were in the hospital. Now you're here with us. Right now you're completely paralyzed, but you may regain some range of motion over time."

Stella blinked. She could hear the words Nurse Green was saying. She could not connect them with herself. But they did explain those white walls, those blue curtains, her no-words, no-moving new world.

"So you're going to stay here with us for a while, and we're going to take good care of you. You don't have to worry about anything—we'll do everything."

But I don't want...

"I know it's hard, but please try not to worry. You've got the best possible care. You have nothing to worry about—just focus your energy on getting better. Can you think about that?"

Stella stared at the cheerful young woman, who had not one single grey hair on her head.

"Now, we must establish some way of communicating. Right now that will be really challenging. Let's start with blinking. Can you give me one blink for yes, and two blinks for no?"

Stella realized she now had a vocabulary of only two words.

"Mrs. Sylvan? Will you blink once for yes if you understand me?"

She blinked once.

"Okay—and do you remember how to say no?"

She blinked twice.

"Great! I'm going to take that as a yes you do remember how to say no: with two blinks. Wonderful. We're going to get along just fine."

Stella blinked once.

"I'm glad you think so too! Okay, I'm going to give you a few minutes to think about all of this. I know it's a lot of information. I'll come back shortly to take you to the common room. It's lovely there—all sorts of friendly folks."

She was gone in a whisk of cheeriness, leaving Stella alone with a mind full of hideously unwelcome thoughts. Then the worst one came: *But what about my dog?*

Chapter 3

SAM

SAM STOPPED WRESTLING WITH HERSELF. She was going to keep this dog.

"I'm going to help you. I'll give you everything you need. Come on..."

The dog wagged his tail.

She didn't have much time. It would be dinner soon, and there was a lot to do. She quickly started up the yard toward the woods where a small shed hid behind the first row of trees. Sam's parents had used it for storage until their garage sale a few months before. Lately it had stayed empty; there was no way

Mom would bother them there. The dog followed her, seeming happy to go inside.

Good. Now nobody would see him.

Sam knew that the dog's strange gentleness would not affect Mom—nothing would change Mom's certainty that large long-haired dogs were dirty and unpredictable and took up too much room. When Mom had agreed to get a dog so that Sam could learn about responsibility and loyalty, she had dismissed Sam's plea for a beautiful big Bernese mountain dog. Instead, they had gotten Piglet, a West Highland terrier. He was wonderful in his own way. Better still, according to Mom, he was small, clean and had his hair trimmed respectably short. But already Sam felt closer to this big black dog than she ever had to Piglet, although she couldn't understand how or why. It felt like she had known this mystery dog for years.

With the black dog safe in the shed, Sam hurried back to the house. Wiping her muddy hands clean on a fern bush, she monkey-glided up the rope ladder, like a spy. She whirled through her room and had it tidy in about ninety seconds.

Bounding down the stairs, Sam shouted, "It's done, Mom! You can check. I'm just going outside for a few minutes."

"Okay..." Mom's voice floated up from the laundry room in the basement.

Good, Sam thought. She should be safe in the kitchen for a few minutes. She found two old plastic containers and filled one with water from the tap and the other with chicken stew from the pot on the stove. Next she filled her pockets with some of Piglet's dog biscuits. She carefully carried the heavy containers to the mud room and looked for the other things she needed.

Sam froze as she heard the front door open and slam. Dad was home. Piglet came yipping out to greet him. Sam heard Dad talking softly to Piglet and then calling out, "Hi, everybody! I'm home!"

She held her breath, hoping he would go upstairs and not into the kitchen. When she heard his heavy thumping on the stairs, Sam unfroze and exhaled in relief. *Yes!*

Her hands shaking, Sam grabbed two old work towels from the basket by the door, and from her school bag she took her hairbrush—she never used it anyway. With the towels draped around her neck, the biscuits in her pockets, the brush clamped between her teeth and a container in each hand, Sam trudged out to the shed.

When she opened the door, the dog looked worried at first, and then he wagged his big bushy tail in circles. Sam put the stew down and the dog stuck his tongue into the container, swooped it around the edges and folded the stew into his mouth. He swallowed the whole mouthful without chewing it. He did that three times, until not a drop of stew remained. He must have been starving, Sam realized.

"I'll bring you more as soon as I can," she promised. She felt a thrill of pride surge through her chest. She was helping him! He had come here for help, and she was providing it.

Now Sam could clean him up. She grabbed one of the towels, rubbing and wiping him until the towel was black. Then she took the brush and worked it through his matted tangled fur until it felt smooth. It must have hurt him, but the dog didn't cry or whine. He stood patiently, not even trying to wriggle out of her grasp. He seemed to understand that he needed to get cleaned up, and he leaned into her hands contentedly.

"You are *such* a good dog, aren't you? I'm so happy you came to find me. I'll take good care of you, I promise. We're going to have so much fun together."

Sam's heart beat faster as she thought about all the sneaking around she would have to do to take care of the dog. It would be the biggest adventure she'd ever had.

Finally Sam was finished grooming the big dog, and as a thank-you he covered Sam's face with huge slobbery kisses.

"Gross! Thanks, boy, I guess," she said, laughing. "I know you mean it as a compliment."

Sam spread the clean towel on the shed floor and patted it. He lay down, curling up and folding his tail over his nose, heaving a huge gusty sigh of satisfaction. Sam put the container of water close by so that he could get it easily whenever he felt thirsty. She emptied the biscuits out of her pockets.

"Here you go. You can have these later, for dessert."

Sam had to go in for dinner. As she opened the door to go, she glanced back at the resting dog. He

looked like he had everything he needed. Because *she*
had given it to him. For the first time in her life, Sam
felt like she'd done every last thing exactly right. The
dog seemed to smile at her again.

"I'm really glad you're here—"

Sam realized the dog needed a name. What was the
perfect name for such a mystery dog? She remembered something her mom liked to say: "There are
more things in heaven and earth, Horatio, than are
dreamt of in your philosophy." After this afternoon,
Sam was beginning to see it was true. She had never
imagined a dog so gentle, so mysterious, before now,
and she had never known that she could take care of a
dog all by herself.

So: Horatio. It was just the right name for the stately
gentle dog. She rolled it through her mouth, to see
how it felt.

"Horatio. Are you okay, Horatio?" asked Sam.

Horatio thumped his tail hard on the floor in
response.

. . .

STELLA

Stella sat in the common room, surrounded by clinking cups competing with chatting voices, the smell of warm coffee and a fresh breeze from the open window. She wondered about her new life here. Her new two-word-vocabulary world. How would she visit with people? What would she *do* all day? She was used to a busy, busy life: volunteering at the homeless people's shelter downtown and walking through the woods with her dog. Puttering and cooking in her little kitchen. Reading her books. Filling her bird feeders and then watching the birds come to feast while she worked in her garden.

All gone.

I can still watch the birds, she realized, looking out at the green trees. *The not-my green trees. I can listen to books on tape.*

But how would she tell Nurse Green that she wanted to do those things? How would she tell her anything?

How would she ask what had happened to her dog?
Stella sat in the breeze and tried to think of a way to
tell about a whole lost life with two blinks.

A few hours later, Nurse Green came back to Stella.
"Did you enjoy your time in the common room?"
she asked.

Stella blinked once.

"Are you all right?"

Stella decided to try something—a third word in her
world. She blinked three times. *Help.*

Nurse Green's forehead crinkled.

"I'm not sure what you mean there, Mrs. Sylvan.
Are you ready to go back to your room now?"

Stella sighed. She blinked once.

"All right. Off we go then…"

This was going to be even harder than she'd
thought.

Chapter 1

SAM

WHEN SHE GOT TO SCHOOL THE NEXT DAY, Sam could hardly swallow. Her throat felt too tight again from the tension of sneaking around all morning, trying to take care of Horatio without her mom finding out. Besides the threat of getting into big huge trouble from Mom for hiding the big dog, Sam was determined to keep him for only herself because it would be something—one thing—that Mom didn't know about.

She'd changed his drinking water and found some breakfast for the dog. Sam did everything as fast as she could while Dad was in the shower and Mom was still asleep. Letting Horatio out of the shed to do his business made her heart pound. He might dash out into the front yard where Sam's mom or some neighbours could spot him. But Sam was lucky. Horatio, so calm, seemed sure the shed was the right place to stay.

All through breakfast Sam jittered as she pretended she was just her normal self, ready to go to school, while all the time her mind was racing out to Horatio in the shed, wondering why he was here, wondering what she would do with him. She had to pretend, though, especially while Dad talked about his big business trip.

"I'll miss you, my Sammy-owl," said Dad, crunching through his toast.

"I'll miss you too, Dad. I wish I could come with you to San Francisco. It would be so cool." She was sure her voice was nervy-squeaky, but Dad didn't notice, thank goodness. Dad was so much easier than Mom.

Sam hugged and kissed Dad goodbye. She would miss him a lot, but one fewer person to hide Horatio from would make things easier. Although Mom was the one it was hard to hide things from. Once Dad had gone, Sam told Mom she'd see her in the afternoon and left for school.

But first she had a detour. Sam had told Mom she was walking to school through the forest path today. That way she could go through the backyard and up to the woods. When Sam opened the shed door for the second time that morning, she saw that the big black dog had eaten all the food she'd left for him earlier.

(It was Piglet's kibble, but Horatio didn't seem to mind chewing up the tiny little nuggets, which must have seemed the size of rice grains to him.)

"Good dog!" Sam called out to him, holding the door open. "Come on, Horatio, let's go do your business."

He bounded out and started running around her in circles, his tail lashing like a crazy metronome. Once he calmed down, he walked around a little bit, sniffing the ground carefully. After he was finished, he went into the shed again and lay down.

She followed him inside, shut the door and leaned against it with a deep sigh of relief.

"We did it! I'm so proud of you for being such a good dog. You'll be fine in the shed until I get home from school." Sam smiled at Horatio, who thumped his tail on the floor before curling it over his nose. "Then maybe I can figure out where you came from and what we should do about you. Or for you. Maybe you'll want to stay here."

Before she left, Sam gave Horatio one big last cuddle. He nuzzled into her, and his warmth went right through her.

At school she worked on her morning lessons like a robot. She couldn't think about anything but the dog. She could hardly wait for lunch, when she would be able to tell Jazzy all about him. Usually Jazzy had all the good stories: Jazzy did fun things all the time, and her life was much more interesting than Sam's. But now Sam had a great story. She wished she could sit with Jazzy, but they had been separated because they talked too much.

Jasmeet Singh was Sam's best friend. On the first day of grade four, Jazzy and Sam had clicked and they'd been best friends ever since, even though by now everybody knew how cool Jazzy was. Then, Jazzy had been new to the school, and her waist-length, curly black hair and sparkly gold earrings had mesmerized everyone. Sam had been quick to see the mischief hiding behind Jazzy's eyes, tucking into one corner of her mouth. *She looks like she's not afraid of anything,* Sam had thought. *I bet she has great adventures...the opposite of me.* She'd never thought Jasmeet would notice her, but Jasmeet had seen something in Sam too, and had invited her to play that first lunch hour.

Sam had been right: Jazzy was lots of fun. She was an only child too, but unlike Sam, Jazzy could usually get whatever she wanted. And when they played silly games with dolls or tried out new ideas that Sam's mom would have frowned upon, like dressing up as princesses, Jazzy's mom usually just laughed and said, "You girls! So clever!"

Sam spent every spare moment she was allowed at Jazzy's house. She felt more alive when she was with Jazzy than any other time. She could hardly remember what life had been like before Jasmeet.

As soon as the lunch bell rang, they snapped together like two magnets and hurried over to a quiet corner of the classroom.

They made a funny pair. Sam knew that next to Jazzy, she was as plain as plain could be. Jazzy was sparkly. Today she wore a blue dress with cowboy boots, and her curly black hair was fanned back from her face with glitter barrettes. Her big, dancing dark eyes made her look like a kitten—she was *so* lucky.

Sam knew that she looked more like a baby owl—Dad's nickname for her. She had rumply, plain brown hair that wouldn't behave for either scissors or brush. No matter how nice it looked when she left her room in the morning (not usually that nice anyway) an hour later it was messy and crumpled and sticking up in places. Sam had a pointy nose and big, grey, round owl eyes. Her clothes were practical and plain, like the grey sweatshirt, jeans and sneakers she was wearing today. People never noticed Sam the way they noticed Jazzy.

But this morning Sam had pink cheeks and bright eyes. She had been making signals at Jazzy all morning, and Jazzy knew there was news. She could hardly wait to find out what it was.

"A *dog* came to my house yesterday!" burst out Sam. Jazzy was unimpressed.

"What? So? You *have* a dog. There are tons of dogs on your street. What's so exciting about that?"

"No, no," said Sam, "this is a big, huge, giant, massive dog, all black with long shaggy hair and big brown eyes and I looked up from reading yesterday and there he was in the backyard. There's something mysterious about him."

"Ohhh..." said Jazzy, interested now.

"Yes!" said Sam. "And I went out to see him, and he was friendly, and seemed nice and smart, and I got the feeling he had come looking for a place to stay, so I hid him in the shed and gave him some food, and he's still there now! He seems really happy there. It's like he wanted me to rescue him."

Sam didn't know how to explain, not even to Jazzy, the strange calm feeling Horatio gave her.

Jazzy's eyes widened.

"But your mom! Does she know?"

"No! I did it all in secret. Plus I fed him and let him out this morning and put him back in and she never found out anything!"

"Wow! What are you going to do now?"

Sam sighed, because this was just what she wondered herself.

"I really don't know what to do next," she said. "But I know he has to stay a secret. Can you come over after school and help me figure it out? You're so much better at plans than I am."

"I can't today," said Jazzy. "I wish I could, but I have my skating lesson, and then my mom's taking me shopping."

"What about tomorrow? You could come over after Guides and then stay for dinner."

"Okay, that's perfect!" said Jazzy. "I'll just check with my mom. But I'm sure she'll say yes."

"Good."

"Where do you think this mystery dog came from?" Jazzy asked.

"I have no idea. Probably he's lost. He was covered in dirt."

"So sad! Maybe he was treated really badly and he ran away from his horrible home," Jazzy offered.

"That's what I was thinking too."

"We should try to find out. We can't decide what to do next until we figure out where he's come from and why," Jazzy said.

Sam was quiet. Part of her didn't want to know.

They had finished eating their lunches and they went outside to play for the rest of the break. After that the afternoon did eventually pass, but to Sam it felt as slow as watching each grain of sand flow through an egg timer. She clenched and unclenched her fists, waiting until she could get back to Horatio. When the bell finally rang, Sam rocketed out of her classroom and shot home along the forest path.

. . .

STELLA

Stella looked away from the birds and watched Nurse Green move calmly around the room. The smiling nurse tidied Stella's room with the same routine each morning: open the windows, make the bed, put away Stella's nightclothes, close the windows, spritz some lavender spray, turn off the night light.

Stella felt the ache of worry for her dog soften for a moment. She let herself relax, just a little bit. But with just one breath, her mind sneaked over into the corner where she held her memories of her dog. As though a film were playing, she watched the images of their first day together unfold.

She'd found him at the local shelter, and the instant she'd seen him, such a tiny fluff ball of black with a little white star on his chest, she'd known he was for her. He had been playing with a ball and tried to roll it to her through the bars of the kennel, inviting her to play. She signed the adoption papers right then and there.

Even though he was such a young pup, he'd been quiet and calm in the crate on the drive home. She'd talked to him the whole way, telling him about his new home, what they would do together every day, what she would make him for dinner. And when they got home and she opened his crate in the kitchen, she'd expected him to shoot out and frantically explore his new surroundings, sniffing every corner, as dogs do in a new place.

But not him. Even as a tiny puppy, he was drawn to people most of all. He'd stepped out of the crate and settled himself happily into her lap, curling up into a ball. He fit there perfectly, and she patted and tickled and rubbed every inch of him. She could feel how skinny he was—no flesh at all on the bird-bones of his ribs, his hair thin and downy, stinking with filth from the shelter. Stella didn't care that he stank. She loved and nuzzled him anyway, and in response he began to make a low whirring sound in the back of his throat. He was *purring*, Stella had realized with joy. She'd never known another dog to purr, although she'd lived with dogs all her life. But then, as she was already learning, there was no other dog in the world like this one. This little ball of life and fluff made her feel like she was the most important person in the world.

The smell of dirty puppy fuzz, the hardwood floor under her legs, the dog's soft coat, all from almost ten years ago, were just as real to her as the birds outside the window today. And it was a relief to think about something other than blinking, other than finding a way to communicate.

Nurse Green was finished. She came over and rubbed Stella's shoulders for a moment. Then she asked, "Would you like to come to the common room?"

Stella blinked twice for no.

Nurse Green smiled again.

"I thought you'd want to stay here with your birds. I'll see you later then."

To Stella's relief, the nurse had somehow realized that she liked to watch the birds. Now there was a bird feeder outside her window.

In a swirl of lavender, Nurse Green was gone, leaving Stella alone again.

Chapter 5

SAM

SAM REACHED THE SHED IN ONLY TEN MINUTES—record time. Horatio bounded out to her the instant she opened the door. He almost knocked her to the ground with his kissy-licking, bumpy-nudging and tail-wagging. Sam felt an unexpected welling rush of love expand in her chest, which burst like bubbles into a fit of giggling. Horatio pranced around her and made bouncy, playful little jumps, laughing with his whole body.

"Hi, Horatio! I missed you!" The dog wagged his tail even harder. It was the best back-from-school greeting Sam had ever had.

"I guess you need to stretch those big legs by now, right?"

More wagging.

She was nervous about taking him for a walk. What if somebody saw them? What if somebody who knew him figured out that she was hiding him? But there was no choice—he needed to get out of the shed.

"Come on, Horatio! Let's go for a walk!" Sam called to him and started up the path. He followed on her heels.

As Horatio bounded ahead, Sam followed and watched the big dog. His tail was like a flag, pointing straight up, waving from side to side, with its feathery plumes streaming out behind him. His ears flicked back to make sure Sam was there, and forward to hear what was coming. His big square paws plunked down surely, one after the other, as he trotted eagerly up the path. He bounced and sniffed and jumped on sticks and chased bugs.

Sam could tell the sniffing was his most important job. As they followed the path, Horatio sniffed down the middle and on either side of it. Sam tried to see what he was concentrating on, but she could only see ordinary sticks, leaves, stones, earth and bushes.

Suddenly Horatio lowered his head even further to the ground and shot over to a small path on the right. He stopped and looked back eagerly at Sam, inviting her to follow. Every inch of him was stretched tight. Something about it made her nervous, although she didn't know why. She had to make him stay with her.

"No, Horatio," she said. "Come back this way."

His whole body drooped, but after a moment he followed her back to the main path. They continued along, and as they came around a bend they saw a little boy lying on the ground crying. His mother crouched next him, talking softly.

Horatio bounded over to the boy, who screamed. His mother leaned over to protect him. Sam ran up to them.

"It's okay," she told them. "He's really gentle. He won't hurt you," she promised the boy. Was she stupid to make such a promise? But somehow Sam was sure she was right.

Horatio leaned into the woman, who started to pat him, talking to the boy. "Oh, he really is a lovely dog." Horatio nuzzled into her hand. "Jason, honey, sit up and see this dog. He's so nice!"

"Too big. Scary!" said the boy, burying his face in his hands. He was only about two years old. He yelped when he brushed his scraped palms.

"He fell just now when he was running," the woman explained to Sam. "Got himself a bit scared."

Sam smiled. "Poor little guy! Horatio will make you feel better, Jason," she said.

The boy sat up warily. Horatio went over to lie next to him, resting his head on the boy's legs. How did the dog know just exactly what to do?

The boy sat very still, his eyes wide, his breathing still jagged from crying. He watched Horatio to see what the big dog would do. But Horatio was calm, and soon the boy ran his chubby hands over Horatio's head and back. He seemed to forget the scrapes on his palms. His breathing smoothed out. The tears dried up in his eyes. In moments he was laughing as Horatio panted and rolled over onto his back, tummy to the air, legs pedalling as the woman scratched his chest.

"Oh, what a sweet dog," she said to Sam. "You're very lucky to have him, aren't you? What's his name?"

"Horatio," Sam answered proudly. In the time it took to say his name, Sam flash-forwarded to a life where Horatio was *hers*. All the things they could do together. All the people they could make happy, like Jason. By the time she had taken her next breath, she knew it was what she wanted more than anything she'd ever wanted in the world. And that it was probably impossible.

"Well, Horatio, thank you so much for coming over to make Jason feel better. And thank *you*," she said to Sam with a big smile. Sam's heart grew two sizes.

Jason was hugging the shaggy black dog. "Ray-sho! Magic doggie…"

Finally the woman said, "Well, we really do have to get home now. Say goodbye to the doggie, Jason." To Horatio, she said, "Thank you for helping Jason to feel better, Horatio. I hope we see you again soon."

"Bye," called Sam, as they walked away.

"Wow, Horatio! That was awesome!" she said to the dog as they walked back to the shed along the main path. "How did you do that? *Are* you magic or something? Maybe Jason's right."

Horatio wriggled all around Sam. She felt frothy bubbles filling her chest. A magic dog! Her dog. Of course he wasn't *really* magic, but...how did he make people feel so good?

Horatio went inside the shed without prompting from Sam. Rushing to his water container, he drank as loudly as though he'd just returned from an all-day hike.

"Okay, boy. You have a rest now. I'll bring you some dinner soon," she promised.

When Sam walked into the house she was instantly blanketed by vanilla warmth. Mom was baking cookies. Sam inhaled appreciatively and then froze. Wait. In the past few months Mom had developed an anti-sugar policy, and there had been no cookies around since. Why now?

Mom was in the kitchen and she called through to the mud room. "Hi, sweetie! Come sit down and have some cookies. I have something I want to talk to you about."

Uh-oh, thought Sam, feeling a tummy ache developing. The bubble of calm happiness that had swelled around her in the woods with Horatio popped. Mom must have found out about the dog, and Sam was going to be in big trouble.

Sam went straight to the table and sat down. As scrumptious as the cookies smelled, Sam's tummy was starting to hurt.

"Well," started Mom, smiling, "I've got some news."

What? thought Sam. *Maybe she wants to keep the dog!*

"You and I are going to start a new activity together!" her mom announced. "We're going to take Piglet to visit a seniors' centre. He's going to be a therapy dog!"

"Oh," Sam said, totally surprised.

Mom ploughed on, as she always did.

"You know how I do my community service with the Neighbourhood League?" Mom didn't wait for Sam to answer. "I realized that it would be good for *you* to be involved in community service too. And anyway, since your only grandparent lives so far away, this will be a great opportunity to interact with the elderly."

Sam couldn't think of what to say. Where in the world did Mom come up with these ideas?

"And it will be so good for Piglet too."

"Piglet would make a terrible therapy dog!" Sam thought of his silly yapping.

"Well he's very friendly, and it might *help* with the barking. And best of all, we'll be helping the seniors so much. You see, they sometimes get lonely at the home, and having new people to talk to and visit would be really stimulating. Also, many of them used to have their own pets, but couldn't take them to the home. So this way they can visit with Piglet, and it will be a little bit like having their own dog again," concluded Mom.

It all sounded great—for Mom and Piglet. Sam still didn't want to go.

"But why do I have to go, Mom? I'm already busy every day. I don't want to do any more stuff."

"Nonsense. I have already explained the benefits. And there's plenty of time in your schedule. What about Wednesdays after Tae Kwon Do and Saturdays after swimming?" said Mom in a way that sounded like a question, but was not.

Sam sighed. She would be busier than ever. She could feel her throat tightening just thinking about it. *And what about Horatio?* How could she take care of him if she were never here? Sam needed an excuse. Homework?

"But what about my homework, Mom?" tried Sam. "With all those activities, I'm worried that I won't have enough time to do homework. And I get so tired."

"You'll have enough time. Plus, this will allow you to work on your scheduling, multi-tasking and time management," Mom said.

What if I don't want to work on my time management? It was no use. It didn't matter that Sam didn't want to do it, that she already felt too busy. Mom's mind was completely made up. Sam dug through her thoughts for the right thing to say. But nothing she could say would make a tiny dent of difference. Mom was shut up like two huge steel doors, and anything Sam could try to say would have as much effect on those doors as throwing pebbles against them. None.

Inside Sam something burst. She stomped her feet so hard her legs ached.

"You always make me do what you want and you never listen to what I want! I'm NOT going visiting with you and Piglet! I won't do it!"

"I'm not sure what all this fuss is about, sweetie, but you ARE going to come visiting with us, and we're going to start this Saturday." Mom's voice was absolutely calm.

There was nothing else to say. Sam roared a loud howl and ran out of the room like an angry elephant. In her room she barred the door with a chair and dove under her duvet cover. Sam curled up into a ball. She wanted to cry, but she couldn't; she just felt jangly and crackly. No position felt right, and no thought was comfortable.

When she could no longer breathe under the duvet, she shoved it off with a grunt. She lay listening. Nothing. Then she heard her mom vacuuming downstairs like nothing had happened. Sam listened to the vacuum until she couldn't stand lying there any longer. Her room was a cage.

Sam's eyes wandered around. She saw the rope ladder still hanging out her window. Maybe she really would run away this time. It would be less scary with Horatio.

As quietly as she could, Sam climbed down and sneaked around to the shed. Horatio was right there waiting at the door, as though he were expecting her. Sam lay on the rough dirty floor and snuggled up with the shaggy cozy dog. She patted and scratched him all over. He leaned into her hands and snorted happily, making a funny noise in his throat. Sam's tummy ache began to loosen, and the feeling of the iron band around her throat did too.

"Why doesn't Mom listen to me, Horatio? Why can't I make her understand how I feel?"

Horatio stayed still and calm against her legs. His warmth flowed through her.

45

"But *you* listen to me, don't you?"

How did Horatio do it? How could he make her feel so much better when nothing else could? Sam wondered if her throat would actually have closed in on itself if she'd stayed in her bedroom. Maybe she would have suffocated to death. That would serve Mom right.

"But now I feel better. I think you *are* magic, Horatio."

He purred.

"What should I do?" she asked him.

Horatio put his huge head on her lap. He looked up at her and his big, melting chocolate eyes seemed to have every answer in the world in them.

"I know...I know I have no choice. I have to go with Mom. But maybe you can help me figure out how to make her listen to me."

Horatio stuck his tongue out and panted loudly. Sam took it as a yes.

Sam sat with him for a very long time, until she started to feel almost normal again. They could run away another time. Besides, Horatio needed some dinner.

"Don't you go anywhere. I need you, Horatio," Sam said as she left to sneak into the house to get his food.

The dog looked back at her, his eyes chocolate puddles.

. . .

STELLA

Stella opened her eyes and there he was. Her dog stood near the foot of her bed, wagging himself silly. He jumped up and put his muddy paws on the white sheets.

"Little one! That's so naughty!" Stella laughed, still calling him by the puppy nickname that sounded absurd by the time he had reached a hundred pounds. "Come on, I'll take you out..."

But when she tried to get up, it all came flooding back. She couldn't move. She closed her eyes against the hot tears, and when she opened them again, he was gone.

Stella blinked. What was happening? She'd been sure he was here. Had she dreamt him?

He'd always slept on her feet, a lump like an oversized hot water bottle, tucked in happily among the quilts and blankets. When she closed her eyes again she was sure she could feel his warm weight pressing down on her feet.

Chapter 6

SAM

On Thursday afternoon Jazzy came over after Girl Guides. She and Sam walked home along the path, stopping at the shed to see Horatio.

When Sam opened the door, the shaggy black giant jumped up and began his greeting dance. He rollicked in bigger circles than ever around Jazzy, who also got showered with kisses.

"Okay, boy, okay that's enough, we're totally slimed now, thanks," laughed Sam, rubbing behind his ears the way he loved.

Horatio stopped licking but kept wagging.

"Oh, Sam, he's so sweet," crooned Jazzy, draping herself over Horatio. "Isn't he, isn't he just the sweetest boy? Isn't he the bestest dog that ever was? Yes he is, oh yes he is!"

Horatio looked to Sam for permission, and she nodded and gestured to the door. Horatio bounded out and up the path.

"Wow, he's really smart," said Jazzy, following the dog.

"Yep."

"Okay," said Jazzy. "Now I get it. I just love him so much already. It's like he understands you and loves you back."

"Exactly!" said Sam. "That's exactly how I felt right from the first moment I met him! It's so cool you think so too."

She told Jazzy about the little boy the day before, how Horatio had helped him.

"Yeah, I can believe that," said Jazzy. "Kind of like magic."

"So, that's why..." Sam took a deep breath. "I've decided to keep him."

"Sam! That's insane! Your mom will NEVER let you."

"I don't care. I'm going to find a way."

They were standing at the split in the path. Horatio looked straight into Sam's eyes and bounded up the path, taking the right-hand fork.

"Come on," urged Jazzy, "let's follow him and see where he goes."

"Well..." hesitated Sam. She still felt that strange reluctance to follow the other path, but she didn't know how to explain it. "I'm always afraid of bumping into somebody we know. Awkward questions. But...he *has* been cooped up in the shed for a few days now. All right, I guess."

They veered right and began walking up the path. Horatio bounded and sniffed, and Sam and Jazzy talked about what to do with the big dog.

"We need a plan," said Jazzy. Making plans was her favourite thing.

"Well, first I really need to get some food for Horatio. I can't keep on stealing food from Piglet. It's not the right kind of food, plus I can't get enough, plus Mom will notice soon."

"Yep," agreed Jazzy. "Let's make that our mission for this afternoon—getting Horatio's food."

"Okay."

"But we..." started Jazzy, and then they rounded a corner and saw Horatio disappear into a cluster of bushes that almost hid a rickety wooden fence.

"What's he doing?" asked Jazzy.

"I don't know," said Sam. "Come on. Let's follow him."

They shoved back the scratchy bushes in time to see Horatio squeeze between some loose boards in the fence.

He was in a small square backyard, standing in the middle of the grass, staring at them.

"Should we go in?" asked Jazzy.

The house looked dark and deserted.

"Ummm..." said Sam. "I don't think so."

Horatio barked once. It was the first time Sam had ever heard him bark.

"I think he wants us to!"

"Well, *I* don't want to," said Sam. The strange feeling grew stronger.

"Do you think this is the house he came from?"

"No!" said Sam.

"But why else would he bring us here?" Jazzy asked the sensible question. Sam did not want to think about it. Horatio *needed* her. He belonged with *her*.

"We can't just go into someone's yard," said Sam. "Anyway, why don't we just go and buy the dog food? That's the plan for today. That house looks creepy."

"It's not really creepy, Sam, just kind of gloomy," said Jazzy. "But I think Horatio is trying to tell us something."

Jazzy was probably right, but Sam didn't want to know what Horatio was trying to tell them. Unless it was that he wanted to stay with her forever.

Sam called to the dog, who stood still, blinking at her.

"Come on, Horatio! Let's go!" she tried again.

Sam and Jazzy backed away into the path. Finally Horatio pushed out through the fence and bounded over to them. He whined and nudged Sam's hand. His tail hung limp, not a flag anymore.

Jazzy said, "We really *should* try to find out where he came from and what happened to him."

Sam stayed quiet.

When they reached the shed, Horatio loped into the small wooden building. Sam started towelling off the mud that Horatio's thick fur had collected during the short walk. He snuggled closer to her and nuzzled his head into Sam's shoulder. His eyes melted into her, full of something. Love for her? Sam felt her chest swell to bursting fullness.

"I don't know how I'm going to do this," said Sam slowly. "But I know for sure we need a really good plan. I *have* to keep him." *He is magic*, she thought. Even Jazzy wouldn't understand that though.

Jazzy nodded. "I can see how much you love him. And I can see why. But..." Jazzy raised her eyebrows and shrugged.

Sam was grateful that Jazzy didn't finish the thought. She checked to make sure Horatio had enough fresh water to last until she came back to feed him dinner. Then she gave him some of Piglet's biscuits from the stash in her backpack. He crunched through them quickly, then went over to his towel bed, circled around and lay down with his signature tail thump. All that was missing was his usual deep sigh of contentment.

He's tired. But he's safe and happy. That's what's important, Sam thought.

"Let's just concentrate on getting his food today, and then we can figure it out from there," proposed Jazzy.

"Okay," agreed Sam.

They went to the house, wondering how they could get food for Horatio. They couldn't talk about it because Mom was waiting for them at the back door.

"Well hello there, girls, you're awfully late this afternoon."

Oops! Sam had forgotten. She thought up an excuse quickly.

"We stayed after Guides to help with the tidying up." Sam tried to look innocent.

"Oh, that was nice of you," responded Mom. "Come and have some brain food for a snack."

Jazzy winked at Sam behind Mom's back, impressed with Sam's new quick thinking. Then she stuck out her tongue. Jazzy didn't like brain food. At her house they were allowed to have cookies and popcorn and sweet tea for snacks. But at Sam's house Mom always made boring snacks.

Today it was carrot and celery sticks with yogurt dip, and brown rice crackers with cheese. It could have been worse. Sam felt like she hadn't eaten in days and gulped it all down so quickly she hardly chewed.

"So what are you going to do for the rest of the afternoon?" asked Mom.

"Well..." said Sam, "we're not sure. I think we'll just hang out in my room for a while, and then decide. What time is dinner?"

"We're eating at six forty-five tonight. Don't be late!" responded Mom.

It was five thirty. They had an hour and a quarter to get food for Horatio. Was it enough time? Sam and Jazzy raced up to Sam's room and shut the door.

"Any ideas?" asked Jazzy.

"Well, I have thirty-four dollars and seventy-five cents saved. Do you think that will be enough?" asked Sam.

"Well, if it isn't," said Jazzy, "I have my emergency twenty in my shoe. You can have it."

"Thanks!"

"Okay, that's one important thing. Now what about getting it?" asked Jazzy.

"We can't ask for a ride. We can't ride bikes. We won't be able to carry a big bag of dog food. Let's walk and take my red wagon."

"Good idea, but we need a good excuse," said Jazzy, the expert plan-maker.

"I know!" exclaimed Sam. "We can say we're going to collect plant samples for a science project. Mom would love that!"

"Good, you're getting better at this! Let's go."

Minutes later they were ready and hovering by the back door, ready to go.

"Mom!" called out Sam.

"What?" Mom appeared from the living room.

"Ummm...we're going to collect some plants for a science project," said Sam.

Mom frowned. "Now?"

"Yes. We *really* need to. It's for homework tomorrow."

"Hmmm...where did you plan to go?"

Jazzy answered, "To the bog at the end of the street. There will be good samples there."

Sam was impressed, as always, by Jazzy's skill. The bog was in the same direction as the pet store.

"The bog? It can be a bit...maybe I should come with you," said Mom, her forehead creasing as she thought out loud.

"No!" said Sam quickly. "We'll be fine. I promise we won't go near the water. We'll be really careful and stay around the edges. We'll only be an hour."

Sam could hear her heart thumping in her ears. Why did it always have to be so *difficult*? Why couldn't they just *go*? She wanted to scream.

"Well..." Mom bit a tiny piece of loose skin on her index finger. "I do have a lot to do. All right. Be CAREFUL! And be back in an hour."

By the time they got back to the shed, Sam and Jazzy were exhausted. They'd had to run all the way to the store. And dragging the wagon back when it was loaded with the huge sack of food was almost impossible. Their hands were blistery. Their legs and shoulders felt like they were on fire. They were covered in dirt and sweat.

"This is kind of what Horatio looked like when he first got here the other day," remarked Sam.

"Ewww," said Jazzy. "Poor thing!"

With their last feeble energy, Sam and Jazzy tipped over the wagon, and the bag of kibble thudded onto the shed floor. Horatio, who had come forward sniffing and curious when they had opened the door, jumped back and whined in alarm.

"It's okay, my boy," said Sam. "Look, we brought some yummy food for you!"

Sam ripped open the huge bag and scooped out Horatio's dinner. He sniffed it cautiously. Then he began to eat, crunching like a dump truck. Halfway through his meal Horatio looked up at Sam. He made the strangest whining, panting noises in his throat. He walked over and licked Sam's chin.

Jazzy said, "I think he's telling you he loves the food!"

"Good," said Sam. "It was all worth it."

"Yep, it really was," said Jazzy.

Soon Horatio lay down on his towel bed, thumped his tail and sighed contentedly.

"Well," summed up Sam, "that part of the plan went perfectly."

They went into the house for dinner.

. . .

STELLA

Stella was lying on her bed. She was restless. She didn't feel like sleeping. Remembering her dog like that had made her miss him so much it felt like a toothache. She was worried about him. Was he hungry? Scared? Hurt?

She needed to find him. She lay still, trying to remember the Morse code she had learned in Girl Guides sixty-four years ago. Maybe she could communicate that way. She thought she remembered SOS: "Save Our Souls." A cry for help. Dot dot dot. Dash dash dash. Dot dot dot. How could she do that? Tiny blink, tiny blink, tiny blink. Big blink, big blink, big blink. Tiny blink, tiny blink, tiny blink. Would that work?

Dot dot dot. Dash dash dash. Dot dot dot. She would try it the next time Nurse Green came around.

Chapter 7

SAM

BEFORE JAZZY WENT HOME they had a rushed, whispered secret session about Horatio.

"Okay, I really think the next thing to do is find out where he came from, so we know if he should go back," said Jazzy.

"I'm pretty sure somebody hurt him," shot back Sam. She couldn't believe she was lying to *Jazzy*. Sam knew it was crazy. But she couldn't let Horatio go back to wherever he came from, not now.

"We don't *know* that. Anything could have happened. Anyway, it doesn't make much sense. Wouldn't he be more scared or angry if he'd been hurt?"

"I think the best thing I can do is give him a wonderful new home."

Jazzy shrugged. "Well, I don't have any more ideas right now." Her face was scrunchy.

"Maybe we'll think of something tonight. Let's make it the last thing we think about before falling asleep. Then we might dream of the perfect plan—how to keep him without my mom finding out. We'll wake up with a great new idea. We can compare notes at school tomorrow."

"Okay, see you then," said Jazzy.

But the next morning, nothing. Even though Sam wanted to keep Horatio more than she could ever remember wanting anything in her whole life, she couldn't think of a plan. For once, neither could Jazzy.

Sam listed the problems she had spent the night thinking about.

"My mom doesn't approve of big dogs, so there's about a one-in-a-million chance she'll let me keep him. Unless some kind of miracle happens."

"Yep," agreed Jazzy, "practically no chance."

"I only get five dollars a week in allowance, so I can't keep taking care of him by myself, because I can't even afford to feed him, not to mention vet bills."

"Yep, you're broke," confirmed Jazzy.

Sam grinned at Jazzy. "You're a big help!"

"Well, sorry," said Jazzy, "I just can't think of anything."

"Hey!" exclaimed Sam suddenly. "*You* love Horatio too. Maybe he could go home with you? Just for a while, until I figure something out. Or convince my mom." Sam grimaced as she thought about how unlikely this was.

"Oh, Sam, you know my parents don't like dogs. It would never work. You know I'd love to if I could."

"I know, I know," said Sam. "I was only hoping."

"Anyway, I looked in the classified ads last night when I got home. I checked to see if there were any lost dogs like Horatio listed. You know—huge, magic, black."

Sam made herself go very still. *Please don't let there be any*, she thought, holding her breath.

"But there weren't," said Jazzy as the bell rang for class to begin. "So we'll just have to keep thinking."

Sam breathed out with relief.

That afternoon she went through the now-familiar process of walking, grooming and feeding Horatio. She could hardly believe that a few days ago she had never dreamt of this dog. Now, being with him was the most important part of each day. It felt like they'd been walking together every day for years.

At the top of the path, they passed an elderly woman wearing a big straw hat. Before Sam could stop him, Horatio started barking crazily and ran up to the woman. She leaped away from him in surprise.

"Call off your dog!" she yelled at Sam.

"Horatio! Stop it!" Sam shouted, shocked. He had never done anything like this before!

But Horatio had already stopped. Once he'd sniffed the woman, he was abruptly silent and still, deflating.

His ears drooped like three-day-old balloons. His tail sagged down between his legs.

"I'm so sorry," said Sam to the woman. "He's really very friendly and gentle. I don't know why he did that."

The woman, quickly getting over her surprise, was friendly now.

"Don't worry, dear. He just startled me. I can see how lovely he is."

She bent over him and began to stroke his back and scratch behind his ears. A smile lit up her face. Horatio buoyed up again and snuggled into the woman.

"Oh, you are sweet, aren't you!" she said to him, continuing to scratch his ears. "You remind me of a dog I grew up with."

Sam watched Horatio transform the woman the way he had done with her, Jazzy and the little boy. Could he affect everyone that way? Maybe even Mom?

The woman said goodbye, and they walked back. At the shed, Horatio lingered outside, sniffing and sniffing. He didn't seem to want to go inside. When he finally did, his eyes were big deep pools. Sam snuggled with the shaggy black dog for ten minutes before she had to get ready for Tae Kwon Do. After that, the promise of the whole rest of the empty Friday evening beckoned. Should she try to talk to Mom about Horatio?

· · ·

STELLA

Mrs. Goodard, the head of Birchwood Retirement Home, poked her head into Stella's room. Stella was sitting by the window with the first spring sunshine filtering through the glass and warming her cheeks, like a stroking hand. She watched the birds flit around the bird feeder just outside her window. Her favourites were the chickadees, and she smiled inside herself as she saw a group of the thumb-tiny brown birds dart together toward the feeder ledge. The birds took turns all day, back and forth, to and from the feeder.

It was Stella's only refuge to watch the birds all day. Her eyes followed a few that must have lived close by as they traced the same paths to their nests with their fluttering wings a dozen times an hour. She couldn't see the nests, but she knew they must be there.

Just like her dog must be there. Somewhere.

She looked away from the window and blinked in greeting at Mrs. Goodard, who had appeared in front of her.

"You like dogs, don't you, Mrs. Sylvan?"

Stella smiled inside and on the outside blinked one huge blink.

Mrs. Goodard beamed a smile so big it almost lit up her butterscotch halo of hair.

"Good. We've got a new dog starting to visit tomorrow. I'll make sure he comes to see you."

Stella's heart clutched with excitement. She thought again of her own dog. *What if he was coming to visit? Maybe somebody found him...*Stella knew she was being ridiculous. Things never happened like that. Especially not in a two-word world.

Suddenly she realized she hadn't tried Morse code on Mrs. Goodard yet. In a dream last night Stella had remembered the rest of the alphabet. She could signal dog now, as well: dash dot dot, dash dash dash, dash dash dot.

But first, SOS. Help.

Dot dot dot. Tiny blink, tiny blink, tiny blink.

Dash dash dash. Big blink, big blink, big blink.

Dot dot dot. Tiny blink, tiny blink, tiny blink.

"Are you all right, Mrs. Sylvan?" asked Mrs. Goodard.

This isn't going to work. Stella wanted to scream with frustration. She blinked once.

"Fine then. I'll see you tomorrow," said Mrs. Goodard. She left the room with a trail of her sweet perfume billowing behind her.

Chapter 8

SAM

SATURDAY AFTERNOON ARRIVED, as Sam had known with dull dread that it would. It was time to go to Birchwood Retirement Home. Her feet moved heavily, like they belonged to somebody else.

She wished she could have stayed with Horatio instead of going with Mom. In the morning she had taken the big dog for a picnic and a walk. When he'd tried to go back to the same creepy house again, Sam hadn't let him. He'd followed her back to the shed more slowly than ever, but he came along with her anyway. Sam felt relieved.

By the time Sam got to the car, the warm magical feeling from the morning with Horatio was gone. Strapped into the seat, a cranky foot-stomping feeling came over her. She was a prisoner in the car, and Mom was starting to lecture about Birchwood Retirement Home. Sam *hated* it when Mom did this. She wasn't a baby. Why did Mom think she needed to explain every stupid little thing?

"All right, Sam," said Mom, warming up to her subject. "I want you to be prepared when we first go into Birchwood. It takes a little getting used to. The first thing you'll notice is the smell. You will probably smell a lot of medicines and antiseptic cleaners. It's not particularly pleasant."

"Fine."

"Mrs. Goodard, Birchwood's coordinator, will meet us," continued Mom. "She will give us a tour today and introduce us to the residents. She's very nice and friendly, don't worry. After today we'll be on our own for our visits."

"Fine." Maybe if she was quiet, Mom would stop.

"And sweetie, the other thing I want you to be prepared for is the residents themselves," Mom carried on. "It might be a bit of a shock. Just keep in mind that each resident has a problem of some kind—that's why they have to live there. Some can't speak very well. Some can't remember anything. Some can't walk or even move. It may scare you at first, but they are just people like you and me."

"Fine," Sam said, hoping Mom was finally finished. *Oh great, this sounds like so much fun,* Sam thought.

The rest of the drive was silent. Sam tried to let Piglet cheer her up. He loved riding in the car, and now he stood up perkily on her lap, twisting and turning to see everything he could through the windows. He helped a tiny bit.

As soon as they walked into Birchwood, Sam noticed the smell. So did Piglet. He shook his little white head and snuffed his nose. Sam couldn't believe she'd ever get used to it.

But then Mrs. Goodard arrived. She was a round, soft-looking woman with fuzzy butterscotch hair curling around her head. Powdery, flowery perfume drifted around her, like she was signing her own signature over the smell of Birchwood. Sam had never seen anyone like her. Even though Mrs. Goodard seemed to be rushing about, taking care of a million things at once, she was calm. She was the eye of her own hurricane. Sam relaxed as Mrs. Goodard reached down and patted her shoulder, her perfume wafting. She blanketed Sam in a huge smile.

"Welcome to Birchwood, my dears," she said, somehow including Sam, Mom and Piglet. "Why don't you just come along with me and we'll have you feeling right at home in no time at all!"

Sam drifted behind Mrs. Goodard, listening to her steady patter of information about Birchwood. Mom seemed caught up in the gentle woman's spell, and

Piglet quietly trotted beside Mom. Amazingly, he didn't bark or make a nuisance of himself at all. Mrs. Goodard seemed to captivate Piglet as well.

"All right, dears, now you know where to find everything," she said, finally concluding her tour. "Let's go to the common room and get Piglet introduced to see how he does. It's been years since we've had a visit from a therapy dog."

Mom said, "I'll start things off, and then maybe Sam can take over."

"That's a lovely idea, dear," approved Mrs. Goodard.

Mom approached an alert-looking resident.

"Hello, I'm Henrietta Hudson. I've come to visit with my dog, Piglet. Would you like to meet him?"

Mr. Baker gazed back at Mom. He worked his lips around his teeth, painstakingly forming his response. Finally he got the words out: "Yes, please."

Sam couldn't believe how slow he was. It could take *all day* to visit all the residents. Her heart sank. She thought of Horatio waiting all alone in the shed. Sam took a deep breath, trying to force the air down her throat and into her body.

Mr. Baker wanted to stroke Piglet, but he couldn't reach him—he couldn't bend over to the floor to pat Piglet.

"Oh dear," said Mom, bewildered.

"Oh yes, I forgot about this," said Mrs. Goodard. "Our last visiting dog was a large dog the residents could reach easily. I suppose the only way they can visit with Piglet is to put him on their laps. Let's try it."

Piglet allowed himself to be handled by the two strangers. Mr. Baker was thrilled to have Piglet on his lap. He smiled tremblingly and ran his gnarled hands over and over Piglet's silky smooth white back. He strained to talk to Mom, who had to lean over and concentrate in order to understand him.

"...had a border collie...named Fly...good dog...happy times..." Mr. Baker was murmuring in happy recollection.

Mrs. Goodard turned to Sam.

"I can see you love dogs."

"Oh yes," said Sam, wondering how she knew. "I love them, especially big dogs."

"I must admit, I'm partial to a bigger dog myself, honey. Much more relaxing they are, generally."

"That's it!" said Sam. Somebody had put a finger on what she'd always thought, what Horatio had proved to her.

"Every single one of our residents loves dogs, and most of them used to have their own dogs. Often one of the hardest things for them about coming to Birchwood is saying goodbye to their pets. I wish they could bring them here, but it's against the policy. The residents are only allowed to bring clothing and photographs when they move in here. It's out of my hands."

"That's awful," said Sam. She thought of having to say goodbye to a pet you loved. Like Horatio. *No, I won't. He came to me. He's mine.*

Mrs. Goodard continued, "I've often wished we could have a dog living here so that the residents would have a companion with them all the time. We have a cat, but it's not the same. Marmalade is only friends with a few of the residents, whereas I find that dogs seem to love everybody. Don't you agree, honey?"

Sam nodded. Mrs. Goodard seemed like a kindred spirit.

Now Mom was talking to a woman who smiled and chatted, but her hands and head shook so violently she could hardly pat Piglet. Mom had to hold Piglet on the woman's lap so he wouldn't be shaken off.

"Poor Mrs. Malone. She just loves dogs. I know she's very happy to see Piglet, even though she might not look like she's benefiting much from it," said Mrs. Goodard. "But she is. Dogs have a wonderful soothing effect here. That's why I have considered finding a dog to live here permanently. But it's so much work to choose a puppy and then there's all the housebreaking and obedience training. It's much simpler to have people like you and your mom visit with your own dog."

"Well," Sam admitted, "Mom came up with the idea. She's pretty excited about it."

"Oh, honey," laughed Mrs. Goodard. "I know just how you feel. It's always such a shock at first. But you'll get used to it. And our residents are rather wonderful, you know—you can find out what interesting things they've done. Once you get to know them, you can have some marvellous visits with them."

Sam was not convinced.

"See that lady in the wheelchair by the window?" Mrs. Goodard pointed. "She was an Olympic long-distance runner. She broke world records. And that gentleman in the striped shirt just over there? That's George Kettlebury, the children's author. Do you know *One Sunny Morning*?"

"I love that book!"

"Well, honey, go and tell him so!" commanded Mrs. Goodard in her reassuring way.

They visited for another hour, meeting all the residents in the common room. Finally Mrs. Goodard said, "I'd like to introduce you to Stella Sylvan. She's recently had a stroke and she's paralyzed. She doesn't have any family to visit her, so she would love to see you."

"Of course!" responded Mom.

"Will she understand? Will she know we're there?" asked Sam.

"It's very difficult to know with stroke victims, dear. I like to think she's aware of everything. I'm sure she understands. I know she'll be happy to see you."

"Okay." Sam wondered what to expect as they entered a small, clean white room.

"Mrs. Sylvan! Here they are! Here are the people with the dog."

Mrs. Goodard wheeled Stella away from the window so she faced them.

Sam saw Mrs. Sylvan blink once, a big blink.

"I knew you'd be pleased to see your visitors!" she said to Mrs. Sylvan.

To Mom and Sam, Mrs. Goodard said, "Mrs. Sylvan blinks once for yes and twice for no. She'll love to have Piglet on her lap. I'll just leave you all alone. Thank you so much for coming! I'll see you next time."

She was gone.

Sam brought Piglet to the motionless old woman, while Mom explained why they were there and that they'd be visiting twice a week. "Would you like us to?" Mom asked.

Mrs. Sylvan blinked.

"Wonderful!"

Sam looked up at the old woman, who suddenly started blinking uncontrollably. Sam recoiled, then felt horribly guilty. Her face glowed with prickly heat.

Mom kept chatting softly for some time, talking about the weather, the news, the book she was reading.

Sam held Piglet. She tried not to think about how it would feel not to be able to move or speak. She had never thought of such a scary thing happening. *It must be the worst thing that could happen to you*, she thought. Her throat tightened. She couldn't wait to get away.

When it was time to go, Mom said, "We'll see you in a few days!"

On the way back to the car, Mom told Sam, "I'm so proud of you, sweetie! You did so well. It will get easier after this first time, I promise."

Sam had to admit that the visit wasn't as bad as she'd feared. Except seeing Mrs. Sylvan.

"I think it was extremely fulfilling!" enthused Mom.

"It wasn't *so* bad," admitted Sam. "I guess it was kind of cool meeting George Kettlebury. And Mrs. Goodard is really nice. But poor Mrs. Sylvan." She shivered.

"I know. It's so tragic. And she has no family! We'll have to do what we can to help." Mom smiled at Sam. "I'm making spaghetti and meatballs for dinner—your favourite. And don't worry about chores or anything for the rest of the day. You can enjoy yourself."

"Okay...thanks, Mom."

Mom just smiled again.

Sometimes she's okay, thought Sam. *Maybe I should tell her about Horatio.*

"I'm going outside to play. I'll be back in an hour."

Sam had lots of time before dinner to walk Horatio, play with him, groom him and give him his dinner. She couldn't believe what a greeting dance he gave her—the best one ever—when she opened the door to the shed. He seemed happier again as he sniffed her over and over, toes to nose. When he thumped his tail as she left the shed, Sam was filled with frothy bubbles. Maybe things weren't so bad. Maybe it would turn out all right.

. . .

STELLA

Stella thought about the afternoon. The dog that had visited made her longing for her own dog stronger. Piglet was too small, too darting—more like one of the chickadees than a real dog. The girl who had brought Piglet in had tried so hard to hold the little dog steady in her lap and the mother had picked up Stella's hand and placed it on Piglet's back, but the dog just wriggled around. He didn't seem to know what to do.

And neither did the girl. Even so, Stella would have liked to talk to the girl and her mother. The girl looked the right age to be a Girl Guide, so Stella had given the Morse code one more try. But the girl had blushed and turned her face away.

Nobody understood. It was time to give up on Morse code.

It was hopeless. How would she get to know new people without being able to talk? She yearned, again, for her dog; he had understood everything without words.

Something about seeing the new people and the dog had jigged her brain. She suddenly remembered what had happened before her stroke. She'd gone as usual to volunteer at the homeless people's shelter downtown. She remembered working in the kitchen, cutting up vegetables for the day's soup. But after that there was just that slow black pit, and waking up at Birchwood.

She remembered leaving her dog in the yard that morning. She hoped that he was okay—that he'd nosed his way out and found himself some food.

But Stella was getting tired of trying to look on the bright side. Her bird feeder-filled, two-word world was just too small. The same questions whirled round and round in her mind, the only part of her in constant motion, like a hamster on a wheel. There would be no peace for her until she knew what had happened to her dog. Maybe he had ended up at the animal shelter where she'd found him as a puppy. Maybe the neighbours had taken him in. Maybe he was...she had to face the horrible thought...dead.

Chapter 9

SAM

AFTER BREAKFAST ON SUNDAY MORNING, Mom said, "Sam, I've just had a change of plans for the day. The Neighbourhood League needs my help. They're attending to a house today for an elderly person who's stuck in the hospital—watering the plants, sorting the mail, that kind of thing. Mrs. Renata was supposed to do it but she twisted her ankle yesterday, so I said I'd fill in. I'm so sorry I have to miss your soccer game this afternoon."

"Doesn't matter," said Sam. A little mom-free time at soccer would be great. She'd be able to slack off. She only went to soccer because Mom made her.

"Do you want to go to Jazzy's? You can go to soccer together in the afternoon. Or you could come with me if you want."

"Sounds kind of boring," said Sam.

"Maybe for you. But I love seeing other people's houses. It's so interesting. And Constance says there's a big book collection in this house."

Sam's interest perked up. A book collection. But still...she'd have more fun at Jazzy's.

"Nah," she said. "I'll go call Jazzy right now."

At Jazzy's the girls decided to spend the morning outside with Horatio.

"Just be back for lunch at one o'clock," said Mrs. Singh, when they told her they were going to the park. "You need to eat in plenty of time before your soccer game."

"We will," they promised.

Sam felt herself fill up with air when they stepped outside Jazzy's house. It was so simple! Sam took big deep breaths. They could just...go. It felt so good.

They played I Spy all the way back to Sam's and were still giggling when they flung open the door to Horatio's shed. But their laughter melted away as soon as they saw the big black dog.

He was lying on his towel, drooping and dejected. His ears were flattened against his head like old dead leaves. He didn't dance over to them.

"Horatio! What's wrong?" Sam cried, her heart beating fast. Was he sick?

The great shaggy dog hauled himself wearily to his feet and plodded up to Sam. He pressed his enormous head under her hand and leaned heavily into her leg. Something was not right with him, but what? He'd been okay yesterday, but...Sam didn't let herself think about his reluctance to go back into the shed. She shoved down the idea that Horatio was lonely.

"Let's go for a walk!" She tried to sound cheerful, but her voice wobbled.

"He's really not himself, is he?" asked Jazzy, who had been silently watching since they had got to the shed.

"Umm...no," said Sam.

"Why? What's wrong, d'ya think?"

"I have no idea."

Horatio perked up a bit once he got to the top of the path. Slowly he seemed to wake up. Sam threw some sticks, and Horatio pounced and sailed back to her with them. Then he stopped playing and started sniffing. It was like he was following a tiny darting bird flying just along the ground. When he got too far ahead of them, Horatio would stop, turn back, watch and wait until Sam was close, and then trot off again, sniffing.

He tried to go up along the right-hand path to that same old house again, but Sam called him back. Jazzy looked at her with questions deep in her eyes, and when they finally turned around and came back again, she said, "You know, I really think we should check out that house again. He *really* wants us to go with him."

Jazzy was right. Horatio had stopped again at the turnoff and was staring at them. He was actually quivering. Sam knew he was worried about something. Maybe he would feel better if they went to the creepy house again. She didn't want to, but he definitely did.

This time, when he pushed through the boards in the fence, Jazzy pushed through right after him. "Come on," she said to Sam.

Sam followed.

The yard was just as empty and just as creepy as before. It seemed like a long time since anyone had been there. The grass was overgrown, and on the clothesline there was a white shirt turning green with mildew. Bird feeders hung everywhere, but they were empty, and there were no birds around.

Horatio circled the yard, sniffing. He darted to every corner. Then he slowed down, as though he hadn't found what he wanted. He walked up to a silver dish lying on the ground and nosed it, giving it a lazy lick. Sam watched him, wondering what he was looking for.

"I'm sure he used to live here," said Jazzy. "Look at the way he trots around. He seems to know where everything is."

"He's always like that. That's just how he is," insisted Sam. "Anyway, there's nobody here. He didn't live here alone. So what's the point?"

"Well maybe whoever lived here went away or something, and he's looking for them. See how he's sniffing everywhere? I'm sure he's trying to find something."

"He's a dog. They sniff things. And anyway, who would ever leave him? He's the best dog ever. I'm sure he ran away from somebody who was hurting him. Probably his girlfriend used to live here or something."

"I don't think so," said Jazzy. "It doesn't make sense. Why does he keep bringing us back here?"

While they were talking, Horatio had gone up to the door and started nosing around. Sam and Jazzy followed him. Suddenly they heard voices. All three of them froze, staring at each other. Then Horatio cocked his head and twitched his ears. Jazzy peeked, carefully, in slow motion, through the window. She drew her breath in so sharply her face went red and Sam could tell she was trying not to cough. Frantically Jazzy signalled for them to get down. Sam grabbed Horatio and ducked. Jazzy put her ear to the door, and after a moment ran in a crouch across the lawn, motioning for Sam to follow.

Once they had ducked through the fence and run down the path, Jazzy gasped and ran her hands through her curls.

"Ohhhhhhhhhh my goodness!" she said, panting. "There were a bunch of ladies in there. I can't believe we escaped!"

"Me neither! Were they creepy, like the house? Did they see us?"

"Sam, don't be stupid. If they'd seen us lurking around, they would have freaked out. We would have been in big trouble." Jazzy gulped more air. "They didn't see us."

"Okay. Well, let's get out of here anyway. We can go to my favourite picnic spot for a while." Sam shivered at their narrow escape.

"I wonder if one of them was Horatio's owner."

"That's crazy, Jazzy. He would have barked or something."

"I guess. But we should try to find out. Maybe we should knock on the front door and ask those ladies about him. They might know something."

"No!"

"Sam, I don't get it. You saw how sad Horatio was this morning. I'm sure he must be missing somebody a lot. Why don't you want to help him find whoever it is?"

Sam crossed her arms. Why couldn't Jazzy just mind her own business? She would never understand how Sam felt about Horatio. Sam didn't know how he could change everything for her, but she was sure he would if he were *hers*. Forever.

"I *am* helping him. I'm giving him a good home. I'm taking care of him."

Jazzy snorted.

"Fine, if you call spending twenty-three-and-a-half hours alone in a dark shed a good home. I think you're being mean, Sam."

Sam couldn't believe Jazzy was turning on her like this.

"No! *You're* being mean! You're just trying to…"

"I'm trying to help you, Sam. You said you wanted my help with a plan. I'm telling you, this is the next step."

"No. You're wrong. Why don't you just leave me alone? I don't need your help anyway."

The look in Jazzy's dark cinnamon eyes was the same faraway, deep-pooled look Sam had seen in Horatio's yesterday when she'd closed the door to the shed. Then Jazzy was gone, disappearing around a corner and into a thicket of trees.

Sam tried to convince herself she was right. "Well I guess it's just us now, hey, buddy?" Horatio wagged his tail, but he looked down the path where Jazzy had gone. "I'm helping you, right? Do you want to come back with me?"

Sam held her breath. She began to walk down the path that led to the shed. After a few steps, Horatio followed. She breathed.

In the shed, Sam poured the dog his kibble, and he quickly gobbled it up. She refilled his water, shook out his towel and gave him a biscuit.

"It won't be long now, Horatio," she told him with a confidence she tried to make real. "I'm going to figure everything out soon. Just wait and see!"

But Horatio went very slowly to his bed, like he wished he were somewhere else instead. Sam scratched behind his ears to make him happy, and he thumped his tail once. He was happy here with her, she told herself. He loved her as much as she loved him.

. . .

STELLA

Early evening sunlight filtered in stripes through the window, painting shifting lines over Stella's still legs. She looked out toward the bird feeder. A brazen cheeky squirrel had driven all the birds away and was feasting like a glutton on the bigger seeds. Stella marvelled at the squirrel's nerve, but she knew it could not keep the birds away for long. They would be back.

She thought of her dog. He was so gentle, but his one fault was squirrel chasing. If he were here now, he'd be up at the window, pacing and barking.

"You silly boy," she always said to him affectionately. "You know you won't catch it! You never do!" She laughed inside, thinking of him.

The squirrel looked over to the window and chattered, scolding as though he could see the dream of

Stella's dog. For a moment it was like he was really there. But no. This time she wasn't fooled.

Stella made a decision as fast as blinking her eyes. If she couldn't make anybody understand her, she was just going to have to get better. It was the only way she could get out of here and back to her dog.

She put all of her energy and thoughts into imagining herself with the ability to speak, just a few words to start, and to move, maybe just one hand at first. She formed the sounds and pictures with her mind.

It would work. She knew she could do it.

Chapter 10

SAM

It was hopeless. By Wednesday afternoon, Sam knew it. There was no way in the world it would work: she could never keep Horatio. Each day he drooped a little more and perked up a little less on each walk. Although it made her feel like a stack of bricks was sitting on her chest, Sam had to admit he wasn't happy. *She* was so happy that he was with her, but *he* wasn't happy. Sam felt like she had found the most precious thing she could ever have imagined, but Horatio seemed to be looking for something else all the time. It seemed all wrong to Sam, that she could be so happy and he could be so miserable. It was like a puzzle that didn't quite jig up. Like if she could just shuffle it somehow, it would fit...

But how?

Sam knew there was only one answer right now, even though she wished she didn't. Horatio couldn't stay in the shed for much longer. He was too lonely and worried. She had to help him. How could she get him out without talking to Mom though? The few times Sam had tried, she couldn't. She just could not do it. She *knew* that Mom wouldn't listen, would never understand. And besides, a part of Sam still loved hugging the knowledge to herself that Mom didn't know about the dog. She couldn't believe she was getting away with it. She had to figure this out all by herself.

By herself. Her tummy twisted as she thought of Jazzy. They hadn't spoken at school all week. But Sam knew she couldn't help Horatio without Jazzy's help. And now, the thought of losing him made Jazzy's absence unbearable. Sam would have to apologize. Jazzy had been right all along.

After Horatio's walk, Sam lay on the floor of the shed with him. It was dim and silent, like a cave. They were safe there, but it was suffocating Horatio. The thought of her own world without him made Sam feel like *she* was choking.

"What can we do, Horatio? Isn't there a way for both of us to be happy?" She sighed. "Should I talk to Mom?"

Horatio stopped making the funny noise in his throat. Sam took it as a no.

Her whole body was heavy.

"I guess you can never really be my dog."

Sam snuggled with him for a long time.

"I promise I'll find a way to make you happy." The noise whirred up in his throat again. "You won't have to be alone all the time in a dark shed."

Sam knew the dog was only wagging his tail because he always did when somebody patted him, but she was sure he understood her. She felt a little tiny bit less sad knowing that he would be happy, the way he had made her feel better so many times. But she wished that helping him didn't feel so horrible. She wished it didn't feel like she was losing the best thing she had ever known.

After working up the courage at school the next morning, Sam sidled up to her best friend at recess. Jazzy was hanging out with a bunch of girls who thought she was really cool; they formed a circle around her and laughed at whatever she was saying. She *was* really cool. When Jazzy saw Sam, she smiled and stood up, telling the other girls she'd be back in a minute. They wandered to a corner of the playground.

"Jazzy, I'm sorry. I was wrong. You were right— Horatio can't stay in that shed," said Sam.

"It's all right, Sam. I know how much you love Horatio," answered Jazzy, hugging Sam quickly. "And it's so hard with your mom..." Jazzy shook her head. "So you're not going to try to keep him, then?"

"No, it's impossible," said Sam. "You were right all along."

"What are you going to do, then?"

"I guess we should check every possibility to see if he's missing from somewhere," Sam admitted.

Jazzy tilted her head to one side and eyed Sam. "I should tell you something."

"What?"

"Umm...I couldn't stop thinking about Horatio and the house he keeps going to. I was sure he used to live there. So I did a bunch more detective work. I looked at the newspaper ads and at the animal shelter again. Then I went online."

"Oh," Sam said, not sure what to hope for. "What did you find out?"

"Nothing." Jazzy smiled.

Sam felt lighter. Her cheeks tingled. "Okay. So nobody's missing him." That made it better, but also worse. Where could he go?

Suddenly an idea sprang into Sam's mind.

"Hey! Mrs. Goodard told me she wants to have a full-time therapy dog to live at Birchwood. She was saying that she's really happy we're coming to visit with Piglet because all the residents love dogs, but they're not allowed to have their own pets there. And then she told me that she's been thinking about getting their own dog for Birchwood, but she doesn't want to deal with a puppy. What if..."

"Horatio would be perfect for the job! Awesome!" finished Jazzy. "This is going to be much better for him, Sam."

"If only I could keep him. But at least this way I'll be able to visit. Okay, how are we going to make this happen?"

"Here's what you have to do. First, you have to figure out if Mrs. Goodard was serious about getting a dog, or if she was just making conversation. Grown-ups do that a lot."

"Well, she *seemed* serious..."

"Yes, they always do. Believe me. But you have to be sure."

"Okay," said Sam.

"Next comes the hard part," said Jazzy. "Getting him there. I guess you're still not going to tell your mom? You want to do a stealth operation, right?"

Sam laughed and made crazy eyes at Jazzy. "Stealth, for sure," she said. "The first thing is that we have to move fast. He's been in the shed too long. He's kind of freaking out. And anyway, I want to get him to Birchwood before Mrs. Goodard changes her mind. But how do we get him there?"

"So you're not going to ask your mom to drive you," said Jazzy, stating the obvious. "And we can't ask my parents either. Can you ask Mrs. Goodard to pick him up?"

"I guess I could," said Sam. "But what if she says no? Or what if she says she doesn't want him? Maybe it would be better if he just showed up there. Then she'd have to keep him."

"Risky! I like it," said Jazzy. "But that doesn't solve the problem of getting him there."

"Well...what about bringing him over in a taxi one night and leaving him there?"

"Brilliant!" exclaimed Jazzy. "When?"

"What if I sleep over at your place on Friday night? We can tell your parents that my mom is driving me over, and we can tell my mom that your parents are picking me up," said Sam, thoughts tumbling into her mind.

"Hey, you're getting really good at this," said Jazzy. "Soon you won't need me at all."

Sam hugged Jazzy quickly. "No, I need you, believe me. Sorry I was an idiot. Thanks for helping me with this."

"Oh, you know I love it! What about this: ring the doorbell, call out goodbye and run around into the backyard. Then you can go get Horatio, go along the path and meet a taxi on the other side of the path."

"Good," said Sam. "That will work. Then I can drop him off at Birchwood, and then take the taxi to your house."

"You'll need more money," said Jazzy. "I'll call some taxi companies and find out how much it will cost. I'll get the money from my parents. Oh, and we also have to check if they take dogs."

"Okay, so find a taxi company that takes dogs," said Sam, "and then we'll book one to pick me up on Friday evening. All I have to do is be there at the right time. Easy!"

"No problem!" said Jazzy.

"I'll write a note and tie it around Horatio's neck. Then when Mrs. Goodard finds him at Birchwood, she'll know why he's there."

"Good," said Jazzy, "we've got it all worked out."

"Thanks Jazzy," said Sam, hugging her best friend. "Now we just have to make it work."

. . .

STELLA

Sitting strapped into her wheelchair, facing the bird feeder, Stella watched not the birds but instead the wriggling of her own fingers. She was concentrating fiercely, willing the motion. She took a deep breath and rested for a moment. This work was tiring, but it was worth it. She was getting there.

She tried again. This time, she was able to make a fist with her right hand and then release it, flattening out her fingers.

She was so excited her chest felt like it was filling with bubbles.

"Whah!" she exclaimed in triumph, without even meaning to. She couldn't believe it. "Whah!" she said again, this time on purpose.

The birds twittered and chirped, and Stella told herself they were cheering her on. She wriggled and wriggled her fingers, made fist after fist with her hand.

Soon she was exhausted. She had to stop for now, but she knew she would keep going, adding more movement and more sound to her world. Soon she would be able to ask somebody about her dog.

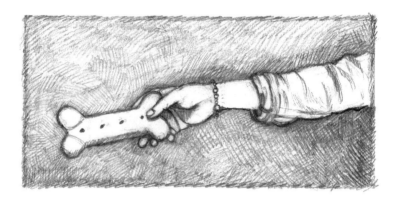

Chapter 11

SAM

THAT AFTERNOON SAM WAS SO BUSY she hardly had time to think about the plan. After school she sprinted home. She only had five minutes to let Horatio stretch his furry legs. She could see how subdued he was, how hard it was for him to be in the shed.

"I'm so sorry, Horatio. That's all I can manage right now. I'll bring you some dinner later," said Sam breathlessly to the drooping dog as she gave him one of his huge, hand-sized dog biscuits. She hugged him and hoped he would be all right all alone.

She was still out of breath as she entered the laundry room door, but luckily Mom didn't notice she was late.

"Hi, Sam!" she called from the kitchen. "Come and get a snack. Hurry now."

Sam groaned. She was exhausted from school and running and rushing to take care of Horatio. She just wanted to curl up on the couch to read, with Horatio's head in her lap. But today they were going to Birchwood again, and this might be Horatio's only chance!

Sam ran into the kitchen where Mom had a plate of brain food waiting—today it was hummus dip with pita chips and an orange. Yum! Sam grinned, and then Mom asked the inevitable: "So what did you learn at school today?"

Sam thought, *That it's better to tell you as little as possible!*

It made her want to giggle, but instead she answered seriously, "Well we're reading *Tuck Everlasting* right now, so we started learning about philosophies of life, and living forever and..."

Mom's eyes glazed over. She wasn't interested. Mom liked science more than philosophy. "Hmm...that sounds nice," Mom said.

When they got to Birchwood, Sam couldn't see Mrs. Goodard anywhere.

"Come on," said Mom. "Let's go to the common room. We can start visiting the residents in there."

Sam followed, scanning all the rooms for Mrs. Goodard.

In the common room Mom said, "Okay Sam, now it's your turn to do the visiting. Remember, if the residents want to hold Piglet, you have to lift him up to their laps. Be gentle!"

Piglet was looking around the room eagerly, his little stump of a tail twitching jerkily from one side to the other, as it did when he was happy. Sam was surprised he liked it here so much.

She decided to visit George Kettlebury first.

"Hi, Mr. Kettlebury," said Sam. She felt a little bit shy. "Remember me? I'm Sam Hudson, and this is my dog Piglet. We've come to say hello and stay for a visit."

His face transformed with pleasure and welcome. Even though he was ninety-four, he seemed like a little boy. His small thin mouth puckered up in a wide grin and his bright blue eyes shone like marbles held up to the light. The skin covering his mischievous oval face was just like tissue paper, thin and fragile, and now it flushed pink with his delight.

"Oh, hello again! It's so nice to see you," started Mr. Kettlebury strongly, hardly betraying a hint of his age. "I wondered whether you would come today, Sally!"

"Sam," said Sam uncomfortably. "My name is Sam."

"I thought this was your day to come with Tiger. Did you have a nice walk over, Sally?"

Sam understood. Sally was the character in *One Sunny Morning*, and Tiger was her dog.

"No, Mr. Kettlebury," pressed Sam, "I'm not Sally, I'm Sam."

"Whatever are you talking about?" said Mr. Kettlebury. "I'm sure I know my own Sally!"

Sam realized there was only one thing to do.

"Of course you're right!" said Sam cheerfully. "I'm just being silly. Silly Sally! Would you like to see Tiger?"

Mr. Kettlebury nodded his small head regally.

Sam lifted up Piglet, who had no trouble pretending to be Tiger. While Mr. Kettlebury patted and snuggled Piglet, he chatted quietly with Sam. He kept calling her Sally, and he talked about things that happened in the book. Sam found it a bit strange, but it was also kind of fun, like a sort of game.

When they said goodbye Sam moved on to visit Mrs. Granger, who was blind. She loved holding Piglet on her lap. Then there was Mr. Jones who couldn't speak at all, but showed how much he wanted to visit Piglet by holding out his arms wide in front of him and smiling.

Out of the corner of her eye, Sam saw Mrs. Goodard walking briskly down the hall outside of the common room.

"Mom! I have to go to the bathroom. I'll be right back." Sam thrust Piglet toward Mom and ran, hoping to catch Mrs. Goodard.

The butterscotch halo of Mrs. Goodard's hair was just disappearing around a corner, and Sam broke into a sprint. She followed the flowery trail of Mrs. Goodard's perfume. But as she caught up to her, Sam had no idea what to say.

"Hi!"

"Well hello there, Sam!" said Mrs. Goodard in a welcoming voice. "You're back again already, dear!"

"Yes."

"And I can see you've gotten over your shock, just as I said you would. Are you having a better visit today?"

"Oh yes!" exclaimed Sam. "First I visited Mr. Kettlebury. He thought I was Sally and Piglet was Tiger. I tried to explain who I am, but then I just gave up and pretended to be Sally."

"Good for you, honey," Mrs. Goodard approved. "It's a bit sad about Mr. Kettlebury. He doesn't live in the real world with us anymore. But I always tell myself he's much happier inside his book worlds. It was nice of you to pretend with him."

Sam smiled and then plunged in.

"Remember you were talking the other day about getting a dog?"

Mrs. Goodard looked a little confused, but she answered, "Yes, of course, honey."

"Well, did you really mean it?" Sam put all her love for Horatio into the question.

Mrs. Goodard flooded Sam with a piercing gaze that took in Sam's rumpled baby-owl-feather hair, her blazing pink cheeks and her fierce grey eyes. Sam stood in front of Mrs. Goodard, her feet planted firmly, her fists clenched. Sam felt like Mrs. Goodard was reading her mind.

"I did. Why?"

"Well," Sam continued, "say there was a really wonderful, perfect dog. Gentle and good and calm, and already completely trained and everything. Would that be the kind of dog you'd want for Birchwood?"

Mrs. Goodard was forced to answer.

"I suppose that would be the ideal solution. But why do you ask?"

But Sam was out of time. Mom might come looking for her any second.

"No reason!" said Sam before turning and running back to the common room, leaving a bewildered Mrs. Goodard in the hallway.

Sam saw a pinprick of sunlight shine into the dark shed where Horatio lay shut away from the world. The plan could really work. It *had* to.

For the next few days, Sam walked and fed Horatio, who was getting more restless each day. At school Sam and Jazzy reviewed their plan over and over, fine-tuning the details and making sure they each had an identical understanding of each step. Jazzy had arranged a pickup for seven o'clock on Friday evening. She also collected thirty dollars from her saved-up allowance to put toward the Horatio cause. They were ready.

But when Sam arrived home from Girl Guides on Thursday, Mom was doing laundry and she held up the picnic blanket. Mom raised her eyebrows and pointed to one enormous muddy paw print in the corner of the blanket. Next to it was one of Piglet's miniature paw prints.

"What is this, Sam?"

Sam's face felt like she had just stuck her head into the oven. She knew that everything from her neck to her ears to her forehead was the colour of a ripe strawberry.

"Uhhh...I don't know."

"Well I do," said Mom. "This is the paw print of a very large dog. The thing I really don't understand is what it's doing on our picnic blanket."

In the few seconds before she responded to Mom, Sam let her imagination speed along in front of her like a sled racing down a snowy hill. She thought about what would happen if she told Mom about Horatio and her plan to take him to Birchwood. Sam tried to visualize Mom helping. Sam wanted to believe that it could happen, but she knew in real life Mom wouldn't act the way Sam hoped.

"Oh, now I remember," Sam lied, "during our picnic the other day, this big dog was walking by and he smelled our food and ran off the path and onto our blanket and tried to steal our picnic. I guess his feet were muddy, I didn't notice. I was just trying to get him away from our food."

"That sounds scary!" said Mom. "Was the dog by himself?"

"No," said Sam, "his owner was there, but he wasn't on a leash. The owner just kept apologizing and apologizing."

Mom's forehead wrinkled. "This dog sounds dangerous. Have you seen him again?"

"Mom! The dog wasn't dangerous. He was just curious about the food. Nothing happened. I've never seen him before or since."

"I don't know...I don't like it." Mom looked hard at Sam. "No more picnics for you for a while, I think. You don't know what could happen with an aggressive dog like that."

"It *wasn't* an aggressive dog! It was just curious. Please, Mom! I love the picnics."

"What's this all about, anyway? It was hard work to get you to play outside until a few weeks ago and now I can hardly get you in. What's going on?"

Sam knew she was still red, and now she could feel prickles of damp springing up on her forehead and neck.

"It's just..." Sam started, wishing she wasn't such a terrible liar. "The spring weather is so nice...I..."

But Mom was looking at her so hard that Sam felt her voice dry up as her throat tightened.

"Hmmm...well next time you want to go on a picnic, I'll go with you. I like spring weather too."

"Fine," she said, and thumped up to her room, wishing her mom were different. Wishing her life were different. She'd thought Horatio would change it for her. But nothing could change her mom. When he was gone everything would be as boring as before.

At six forty-five on Friday evening, Sam silently opened the front door, reached her arm around the door frame, and pressed the doorbell.

As its ringing tone sounded through the hall, Sam just as silently closed the door, slung her backpack onto her shoulders, and called out, "Mom, that's the Singhs. I'm going!"

Her hands were shaking, and her heart felt like it was stuck in her throat. This was the moment the whole plan could fall apart. If Mom wanted to come and talk to Mrs. Singh, it would all be over. Sam would be in big, huge, skyscraper-sized trouble. The two mothers had already talked on the phone, so she shouldn't need to, but she'd been watching Sam so closely lately...

"All right...see you tomorrow morning at ten o'clock!" came back Mom's voice like an echo.

The breath Sam exhaled was jagged and shaky. *Yes! Thank goodness*, she thought as she ran out the door, slamming it extra hard in her anticipation. She ran like a greyhound to the shed.

Sam flung open the door and shouted, "Come on, Horatio! This is going to be the best night of your life! You're getting out of here!"

He couldn't understand her words, but the big dog danced at Sam's tone. He pranced in circles, licking her hands and chin in affection each time he whirled by her. He looked like he was smiling.

Sam fed Horatio quickly. Then she filled a plastic bag with kibble and jammed it into her pack. It would get Horatio through a day or two.

Sam moved her things to one side and fitted in Horatio's towel bed, brush and box of cookies on the other side. Last, she carefully placed the letter explaining Horatio's situation on top of everything. She would tie it around his neck when she dropped him off at Birchwood.

"We're almost there, Horatio! You're going to have a new home. You're going to love it. You'll get to visit with people all the time."

Sam's tummy ached with sadness that he was going, but at the same time, her heart fluttered. They were getting so close. She tried not to think of how much she would miss him.

"Let's go, Horatio. Walkies!"

They bounded up the path together.

It didn't take long to get through the path and out to Percy Street. The street was deserted. Sam could hear distant shouts of children playing a noisy game, and she could smell the mouth-watering scent of something cooking on a barbeque, but she couldn't see anyone. She and Horatio hung back at the edge of the path just in case. Sam scanned the street, anxiously waiting for the taxi cab.

Finally it arrived. The cab driver looked confused. Sam saw him glance down at a scrap of paper before he stopped the car and turned off the engine. Then she felt safe enough to come out and approach the cab.

"Hi, I'm Sam," she said to the driver. "I arranged a pickup to take my dog to Birchwood Retirement Home."

"Nobody told me it would be a kid!" he exclaimed. "And nobody told me the dog would be a bear!"

"But I checked to make sure you take dogs," she argued. "And I am eleven years old."

"Well *dogs*, yes, but *bears*, I don't know."

"He's really good, I promise. Besides, it only takes ten minutes to get to Birchwood. Nothing can happen!"

"Oh all right," agreed the cab driver. "I'm here now anyway."

Sam felt a quick spark of triumph.

"Okay, come on, Horatio. Let's go in the car!"

The only part of the big dog that moved was his ears, which flattened down onto his head. He stared at Sam. She felt a trickle of anxiety twinge in her stomach. She went and sat in the back of the cab, patting the seat.

"Come on, buddy, come on!"

Horatio still didn't move. Sam shuffled over and patted the seat invitingly.

"We're going to your new home, Horatio! Get in the car so we can go!"

But no amount of pleading, begging or cajoling would move Horatio.

Finally the cab driver said to Sam, "Look, I gotta get going. Either you get the dog in, or I'm out of here. Do you want me to lift him up?"

"Well..." said Sam dubiously, "I guess you could try. But I doubt it will work."

It didn't. Worse, Horatio was frightened by the man's rough handling and ran back into the woods.

"Sorry, kid, no luck," said the cab driver. "I can't stick around. You're lucky I'm not charging you for my time here," said the driver grumpily.

Then he climbed into the car and left Sam standing alone on Percy Street.

She turned slowly and trudged back toward the path. How would she get Horatio to Birchwood now?

Sam moved into the thickly wooded part of the path, and Horatio bounded out of the bushes in front of her. He was panting a lot, and he darted in skittish zigzags down the path toward Sam.

"Horatio! That was your big chance! What are we going to do now?"

For tonight Sam was stuck. She had to get Horatio back into the shed. Then she had to be at Jazzy's, or else their parents would figure out something strange was going on.

Sam and Horatio made their way slowly toward the shed. This time, Horatio seemed a bit less reluctant to go inside. Sam opened her backpack, unpacked it and laid out Horatio's towel bed. He circled around, curled himself up, thumped his tail and sighed.

"I'm sorry you're so sad. But why wouldn't you get into the taxi? Why did you come back here if it makes you so sad?"

Horatio didn't answer. He didn't even thump his tail.

Sam shut the door and began the long walk to Jazzy's house. If he was so unhappy in the shed, why wouldn't he leave? *Maybe he wants to stay with me...*But Sam couldn't hold the thought.

She knew one thing for sure—Horatio couldn't stay in the shed for much longer. No matter how much she wanted to keep him, it wasn't the right place for him. Besides, Sam couldn't keep up all this lying and sneaking around. She felt like she was just waiting for Mom to catch her. She would have to find another way to get him to Birchwood. Soon.

. . .

STELLA

Stella worked on the *D* sound. It was a hard one, because she had to curl her tongue up into the roof of her mouth and then pull it back down again. *G* was hard too, clenching in the back of her throat. But she knew that soon she would be able to say "dog." Soon she would be able to ask about her dog.

She had already surprised the nurses with her new words: whah and meh. Although they didn't really mean anything, Stella kept saying them over and over, just to practise. To show people that she was trying. She was happy Mrs. Goodard had asked the speech therapist to visit her, and the physiotherapist too. They were coming tomorrow for the first time.

I'm getting there. Just wait for me, Little Bear, she thought.

A perfect image of her dog plummeted into her mind: he was running up the path next to her, regal and shimmering black, his tail a flag, bouncing and happy as any living creature could be. He was always so *alive*, her dog.

The image promised her that he was still alive, waiting for her.

"D...D," said Stella.

She bounced her hand onto her leg in celebration.

Chapter 12

SAM

AT JAZZY'S HOUSE they tried to figure out what to do next.

"I guess we need a Plan B," said Jazzy.

"Oh...I really thought Plan A was going to work! It was such a good one."

"How could we have known he would be afraid of cars?" asked Jazzy. "But now that we know, it changes our plan a lot. I guess we can't use a car at all."

"We couldn't *walk* to Birchwood, could we?" asked Sam.

"It sure would take a long time," said Jazzy. "Definitely more than an hour. But less than two, I think."

"I *guess* we could walk for that long."

"The best thing about dropping him off on Friday evening was that hardly anyone would be around," continued Jazzy. "Do you think Horatio can wait until next Friday?"

"No way," said Sam. "Not a chance. He went back into the shed fine tonight, but I think that was because he was tired and scared. Every day he gets sadder and sadder in the shed."

Sam pictured Horatio, curled up on his ragged towel in the dark shed, bored and lonely. He deserved a better life; she knew that for sure now. Sam's eyebrows creased together as she concentrated.

"No, he can't wait. We have to get him out this weekend."

"All right," said Jazzy. "That leaves Saturday afternoon or Sunday morning."

"Let's try for Sunday. I'll sneak his stuff into Birchwood when I visit with Mom and Piglet tomorrow. Then we just have to get Horatio there on Sunday. Maybe we could skip soccer. We can take a taxi back to my house afterward," said Sam, planning as she spoke.

"Great," replied Jazzy. "So are you going to talk to Mrs. Goodard about bringing Horatio?"

"I guess that's the best thing to do now," said Sam reluctantly. It would have been so much easier just to drop off the big black dog. But maybe talking to Mrs. Goodard would give Horatio the best chance.

"Yep," said Jazzy. "From what you've told me about her so far, I think you have a really good chance of her saying yes."

"Let's hope so." Sam sighed.

Sam and Jazzy spent the rest of the evening fine-tuning the new plan. They went over every detail until they were as confident in it as they had been in Plan A. Sam hoped they wouldn't need a Plan C.

On Saturday morning Mrs. Singh and Jazzy dropped off Sam early. She had plenty of time before she had to leave for swimming lessons. Sam dropped her backpack outside the laundry room door and zipped around the side of the house, up the path and toward the shed. She tried to make herself as stealthy as a breath of air. Anyway, Mom would probably be in the kitchen, and she wouldn't know that Sam was back yet.

Horatio was curled up on his towel when Sam opened the shed door. He raised his head wearily. Only the tip of his tail twitched. Sam's heart clutched and thudded down into her tummy.

"Hey buddy!" she called, trying to sound cheerful. "Horatio! It's walk time!"

The big dog looked at her, but stayed still. It seemed like an hour before he lumbered to his feet.

"Don't worry, Horatio. You'll be out of here soon," Sam promised.

At Birchwood that afternoon, Sam managed to sneak away from Mom and Piglet again. She found Mrs. Goodard at the front desk, chatting with the receptionist.

"Hello, Sam!"

"Hi, Mrs. Goodard. Ummm...I have something really important to talk to you about."

"All right," said Mrs. Goodard. "Let's sit down. What's on your mind?"

"Well, remember we've talked a few times about finding a dog to live here at Birchwood?"

"I could hardly forget."

"I think I've found the right dog."

"I'm all ears," said Mrs. Goodard, leaning forward.

Sam described Horatio, and then she told the whole story of how he'd found her. She left out the part about the shed, concentrating on convincing Mrs. Goodard that Horatio needed a home, and that he would be the perfect dog for Birchwood.

"So what do you think? Would you let him live here?" she asked when she had finished. She could hear her heart thumping in her ears.

"My goodness, Sam! It sounds like magic. And Horatio sounds like a dream dog. Well, we can try it out. From what you say, I think he'll fit in very nicely here."

"That's great! I know he will. You'll be so happy you let him live here!" Sam had to keep herself from shouting.

"Yes, I think the residents will love him," said Mrs. Goodard.

"They will! They will! I promise."

"Well, off you go then, sweetie. Why don't you bring Horatio in tomorrow morning?"

Sam skipped down the hall.

. . .

Stella

"Excellent, Mrs. Sylvan!" the speech therapist said, her voice filled with praise. "That was an amazing session. I can't believe how much progress you've made in only one hour! Now, in the next few days, I want you to practise everything we've gone over today. Okay?"

"Yuh," said Stella. She could feel her lips curving toward a miniature half-smile. A real smile!

"Great. I can't wait to come back and see how well you've done."

"Meh tuh," agreed Stella.

"All right, so I'll see you Monday, then. Bye!"

The speech therapist left Stella's room. But she almost bumped into Nurse Green in the hall. Stella overheard their short conversation.

"Well how did it go with Mrs. Sylvan?"

"It was very promising," said the speech therapist. "I can tell you right now that the patients I've worked with who have made that much progress so quickly after their strokes have all made impressive recoveries. I have a very good feeling about Mrs. Sylvan."

"Wonderful! I'm so pleased to hear that," said Nurse Green.

"But, there was one strange thing. She did seem fixated on certain letters. I'm not sure if she's still a bit confused, or if she was trying to tell me something."

I'm trying to tell you something! thought Stella in her room. *Oh, I'm trying so hard to tell you something...*

Chapter 13

SAM

SAM COULDN'T BELIEVE she had actually enjoyed the day's visit to Birchwood. After hearing the wonderful news about Horatio from Mrs. Goodard, Sam had gone back to the common room to find Mom and Piglet. Mom was deep in a conversation with the only married couple living at Birchwood. She didn't want to leave, and she said to Sam, "Why don't you pop over to Mrs. Sylvan with Piglet? She'll love seeing both of you. Come back here when you've had a good visit."

Sam couldn't believe the change in Mrs. Sylvan.

The old woman greeted Sam by saying, "Huh!" and lifting up her right hand slightly in a version of a wave.

"Hi, Mrs. Sylvan!" exclaimed Sam. "Wow! You're doing so much better!"

Mrs. Sylvan was actually able to smile back. It transformed her into a completely different person, Sam thought.

"We came to say hello. Would you like to see Piglet?"

"Yuh," answered Mrs. Sylvan.

Now that Mrs. Sylvan had little morsels of movement and speech, Sam felt less awkward around her, and less scared of her too. They could talk, a bit.

"You really like dogs, don't you, Mrs. Sylvan?" Sam asked.

"Yuh!" Mrs. Sylvan smiled again, and then shook her head slightly, the most she could manage. "Buh duh. Buh." She held up her arm.

Sam stared. What did Mrs. Sylvan mean?

"Meh duh," the old woman continued, pointing at herself. "Luh Buh."

She pointed at herself.

Sam tried to put together these strange clues. The words made no sense—they weren't even words—and the arm motions didn't seem to...

"Oh! You used to have a dog? Is that right?" Suddenly Sam saw how Mrs. Sylvan's communication fit together into a message.

"Yuh! Yuh! Meh duh! Luh Buh!"

A tear slid down Mrs. Sylvan's cheek, but she was smiling.

"You had a dog. You must miss your dog so much," said Sam. "I hope visiting Piglet helps."

Mrs. Sylvan smiled again.

When Sam left, she felt different. She couldn't believe she had been afraid of Mrs. Sylvan. And look what the old woman had done. Learned to speak and move again.

After dinner Sam lay on the couch, reading. She had fed Horatio and settled him for the night. The house was quiet. Mom was puttering in the kitchen.

Then Sam heard a loud yell and thump from the backyard. She ran to the window. Nothing. What was it? Suddenly Mom came striding down into the yard from the shed. She disappeared around the side of the house, and Sam heard the laundry room door slam. She stood at the window, completely frozen. Her mind went blank.

Mom was in front of her in seconds. Her eyes were set like stones. She put an iron arm around Sam's shoulder and marched her out to the shed. Horatio's towel and dishes were there, along with his kibble. A cardboard box filled with old kitchen gadgets lay tumbled on the floor.

"Where's Horatio?" Sam blurted.

Mom looked at Sam and shook her head. "You have some serious explaining to do. Let's go in the house and you can start from the beginning."

"But..."

"Move!"

They sat at the kitchen table. Sam asked again, "Where's the dog?"

"Sam, before I tell you anything, I want *you* to tell *me* exactly what's been happening. Why was there a dog in the shed? Where did it come from?"

Sam knew she had no choice. She told her everything.

"I cannot believe you've been hiding a dangerous beast in my shed for weeks! And lying to me and sneaking around!" Mom's voice became more shrill with each word. "I would never have believed you were capable of this, Sam. It's outrageous behaviour."

Mom crossed her arms in front of her chest, shaking her head.

"But Mom...I had to help Horatio! He's..." How could she ever have thought, even for one second, that Mom would understand? How could she explain the way the big dog made her feel? "Magic," Sam concluded in a tiny voice. She knew it was no use.

Mom snorted. "I very much doubt that mangy old mutt is...Anyway, that's beside the point. If you were trying to be helpful, Sam, you went about it entirely the wrong way. The end never justifies the means. It doesn't matter how good your reason is—it's never an excuse to sneak and lie. And what on earth made you think you could deal with a humungous, unpredictable stray dog on your own?"

"I'm really sorry," said Sam, trying a different strategy. "I'll never do anything like that again, I promise. Can you *please* just tell me where Horatio is?"

"Where he is? Where that filthy creature is? I have no idea. He ran away into the forest before I could get him. I'll call Animal Control and they'll take him to the pound."

"Oh, Mom! No! He's supposed to..."

"Supposed to what?" asked Mom, arms still crossed.

"He's supposed to be moving in at Birchwood tomorrow. I arranged it all with Mrs. Goodard. She wants a live-in therapy dog, and Horatio is the perfect dog for the job."

"That mangy old mutt? A live-in therapy dog? What a ridiculous..." Mom hissed a sigh out through her teeth. "Oh, Samantha, you really have created quite a situation here."

No, fumed Sam, *you created the situation*. If only Mom had waited one more day to take that junk out to the shed. If only she would listen.

"I have to find him, Mom."

"You must be joking if you think you're going anywhere. Animal Control will find him and deal with him the way he should have been dealt with in the first place. *You* are grounded. You're not going anywhere but to school and activities for the next two weeks, and no talking on the phone either. You can go to your room now."

"But Mom! I—"

"Samantha! I will figure out how to fix this mess. I'll call Birchwood." She glanced up at the clock and exhaled a frustrated burst of air. "It's too late. Mrs. Goodard will be gone. Well I suppose it can wait until the morning." She glared at Sam. "Get up to your room, now."

Sam was filled not with ants or anger or elephants or stomping. She was just numb with dread about Horatio. She trudged to her room and lay motionless on her bed, trying to figure out what to do.

. . .

Stella

Stella knitted her fingers together, loving the feeling of each finger furling and curling. She separated them and laid each hand on the armrest of her wheelchair. Then she did it all again, twice. She could really feel her hands now.

And she could almost feel her dog lying beside her.

The speech therapist had said she was going to recover. Stella was even more determined now to keep working and working until she was allowed to go home. It was a wonderful thought—an amazing thought—and one that hadn't really crossed her mind until she had heard the speech therapist talking.

She would go *home*. But what would she find there? Would her dog come back to find her? Was he gone?

She promised herself that tomorrow she would make somebody understand her words, her question about her dog.

Chapter 14

SAM

THE BLUE LIGHT OF HER CLOCK flickered and flashed. Midnight. Time to go. Sam reached under her bed for the backpack full of supplies she'd filled it with earlier, slinging the pack over her shoulders and smoothing down her coat. She pulled out her boots and the rope ladder too.

She tried to make no sound as she crept over to her window and slid it back. But her breathing seemed like a thunderstorm, and the tiny creak and buzz as the window opened was like a wrecking ball hitting the whole house. She couldn't believe Mom wouldn't wake up.

Just in case, Sam froze and waited a few minutes. Nothing. The house stayed silent. Before she knew what she had done, Sam was down the ladder and heading into the forest. She had to find Horatio, and she was sure she knew where he'd be. Her flashlight's thin circle of light seemed like the only thing in the huge dark world.

Sam had walked this familiar path a million times during the day, but everything was different in the darkness. Her heart was beating so hard she thought it might thump right through her ribcage. She couldn't remember ever being this scared in her life. She didn't even know what to be more scared of: what Mom would do when Sam eventually went home, what might happen in the huge dark woods or the fact that she was going to the creepy house.

She shivered. Everything in her body was pulling her back to her soft safe bed, but Sam knew she had to make herself keep going. She pushed each foot forward and down, over and over, and finally, after what seemed like hours, pushed herself right through the loose fence boards, through the bushes and into the backyard of the old house.

A black shape somersaulted toward her.

"Horatio! You're here! I knew it! And you're all right. Thank goodness."

The big dog graced Sam with his full-out, happy dance greeting: tail-wagging that shook his body, circle jumping and wet sloppy kisses all over Sam's legs, arms and face. In turn, Sam ran her hands all over him, rubbing, scratching, patting and thumping. She was sure his fur had never felt so soft. She had seen him only a few hours ago, but it felt like he'd been gone for weeks. He felt so solid that she forgot to be afraid of the empty night, and her chest filled up with bubbles because she had found him.

Not that there had ever been any doubt that she would. She'd known exactly where he would be.

Just as she knew what they were going to do next. They would go into the house. As scary as it might be in a stranger's dark empty house, it couldn't be worse than spending the night outside. And she couldn't go home—this was the only way she could get Horatio to Birchwood in the morning.

"Okay, buddy. Help me out here. Let's go inside."

With Horatio sticking so close that he was almost stepping on her feet, Sam checked every door and window to see if anything was unlocked. No luck. She checked under a flower pot beside the door and under the mat. No key—nothing.

"Now what?" she whispered. This was beginning to seem like a very bad idea. Why was she even trying to get into the house? What if someone lived there; what if they were still inside? Maybe she should just go home.

Horatio whined and nudged her.

"I'm sorry, boy. I just don't know what to do now."

Horatio nudged her again and stuck his nose in the garden bed beside the back door.

"What is it, Horatio?" Sam shone the flashlight where Horatio was pointing. A stone turtle was half hidden beneath a bush. She picked it up, suddenly hopeful, but there was nothing underneath. As she put the turtle back down though, she felt its shell move. It was a lid! Inside the tiny compartment was a single silver key.

"You knew, Horatio! You knew where the key was!"

She opened the back door and Horatio danced into the house behind her. Jazzy had been right. This *had* been the dog's home. He knew exactly where he was going, trotting purposefully up to the kitchen. With only the flashlight to shine through the deserted house, Sam felt the shadows all around pushing into her. If she hadn't been with Horatio, she would have run back home.

It's just one night, Sam promised herself. *I can do this. For Horatio, I can stay here for one night.*

In the kitchen, Horatio walked over to a cupboard and stood staring at it. Then he looked back at Sam, staring purposefully. In spite of her fear and worry, Sam had to laugh.

"Okay, Horatio! I guess you must be hungry after all that."

Sam was right. It was the cupboard with his dish and kibble. This was his house. So where was his owner? Sam didn't want to think about that. She filled the bowl and watched while the dog quickly gulped down the food. Then Sam re-filled the bowl with fresh cold water. He slurped noisily, and then just as purposefully, turned to trot out of the kitchen. Horatio was as completely at home as Sam was bewildered.

"Where are we going?" she asked him.

He led her down a dark narrow hallway and into a small square room. She turned a desk lamp on. All four walls were lined with bookshelves, and all the bookshelves were filled with books.

In the middle of the room were two saggy, comfortable old couches. Without hesitation, Horatio jumped up onto the saggier one, curled up, covered his nose with his tail and sighed.

"Horatio! That was what you wanted all along? Your couch? Okay, well at least you're happy now," said Sam. She scratched behind his ears and down his back the way he loved.

Then Sam looked around. The books on one wall were much more colourful than all the rest. Looking closer, she saw that they were children's books. Sam didn't feel like sleeping—she wasn't even sure if she *could* sleep in this empty dark house—so she wandered over to the bookshelf. She ran her hands along the dusty wood. She had never seen so many books in some-body's house. Some of the spines were rough cloth— old books— and others were smooth cardboard—newer books. She saw the Anne books, *Black Beauty*, *Little Women*, *The Incredible Journey* and lots of her other favourites too. Sam opened several that were inscribed with a wobbly "Stella." Some books were *really* old—Sam found a copy of *Alice in Wonderland* from 1911.

She grabbed a handful of the most interesting-looking books and piled them on the couch next to Horatio. Before settling down with them though, she just had to look at some of the other books. The bottom row of shelving on the opposite wall was filled with big heavy books. Sam pulled out a huge atlas, marvelling at the colourful fold-out pages. She looked up France, where she'd always wanted to go.

Another big book caught her eye—*Gentle Giants: Dogs That Changed the World*. It thudded out onto the floor, and Sam flipped through pages of shaggy brown dogs pulling carts and big black dogs rescuing drowning people. The dogs looked like Horatio's distant cousins. When Sam turned a page near the end of the book, a small photograph fell out, upside down. "My Little Bear" was written on the back, in the same wobbly writing that spelled "Stella" in the old books.

Sam picked up the photograph. She turned it over. Staring up at her was Horatio. Sam's breath stuck in her throat. A hundred thoughts swirled around in her mind. Little Bear. Stella. Mom helping out at a house with the Neighbourhood League for an elderly person who'd gone to the hospital. Mrs. Sylvan at Birchwood Retirement Home telling her she'd had a dog. Stella Sylvan. "Luh Buh."

Sam looked up at the bookshelves. She had been too interested in the books to pay attention to the shelf cluttered with framed photographs, but now she stood up and took a closer look. The first picture she saw was of Horatio with a laughing silver-haired woman. She didn't look much like Mrs. Sylvan. But in the next picture the woman wasn't smiling, and Sam could see that it was the same woman she had met at Birchwood.

Horatio was Mrs. Sylvan's dog.

Sam pieced it all together like a jigsaw puzzle. He must have been in the yard when Mrs. Sylvan went to the hospital. That's why he kept returning—to see if she'd come home. Poor Horatio! No wonder he'd been so anxious.

But what about Mrs. Sylvan, Sam wondered. How horrible for her! She hadn't been able to talk. Even now that she was recovering at Birchwood, she was still trapped inside a motionless body. She couldn't ask about Horatio—Little Bear. If she loved him even half as much as Sam did, she must have been frantic with worry. Sam remembered the tear on Mrs. Sylvan's cheek when she said "Luh Buh."

"Horatio! Little Bear! I know what you've been looking for. Or *who* you've been looking for. It's Stella! I'll take you to her tomorrow, I promise."

Although he couldn't have understood, Horatio thumped his tail.

Sam could hardly wait for the morning. Now it was just a matter of getting through the night.

Sam went back to the couch. She put the photograph in her pocket and spread the books out. Horatio lay curled at her side. All night long she read the books, with the light from the lamp opening up the adventure-filled worlds inside them. She kept her arm around Horatio, and in the back of his throat he purred his happiness.

· · ·

STELLA

Stella couldn't help it—there were so many quiet, still moments in her long days that she couldn't help thinking about her dog: where he was, what had happened to him. She forced her mind to remain positive. He was alive. Somebody kind had found him and recognized his gentle magic; somebody loved him and was taking good care of him. But how far away was he? How would she ever find him again?

Since the speech therapist's visit, she had made herself stop wondering. Instead she put her energy into practicing the words that would help her move closer to him. She moved her mouth around the sounds, sometimes just in her imagination, sometimes really pushing the muscles.

She was getting there. Stella made a plan, step-by-step, in her mind. First she would ask Mrs. Goodard to call the animal shelter and find out whether Little Bear was there. If he wasn't, she would request help with placing a lost ad in the local paper and putting up posters around the neighbourhood. Somebody would know where to find Little Bear.

Once he was found, she could begin the last steps in her plan. Stella would go home with him, and they would begin to live their life together again. Then finally they would start coming to Birchwood every day so that her dog could use his magic to help everyone there.

Chapter 15

SAM

HORATIO WAGGED HIS BUSHY TAIL, but he refused to follow Sam out of the yard. She had woken up at first light and was determined to get to Birchwood as soon as it opened.

"Come on, boy! Come on, Little Bear. Let's go see Stella!" she cried.

No amount of coaxing could convince the dog. He wouldn't budge. In frustration, Sam resorted to pushing and pulling him. She snapped on his leash and dragged him along behind her. She felt horrible, especially when he started yelping and trying to turn back.

"We're going to see Stella," she kept telling the dog. "I promise. You'll be so happy. Come on!"

It took a long time to reach Birchwood.

But as they walked, even though she was straining to move Horatio along with her, Sam felt how beautiful the morning was. The whole world seemed like a new place. The sun shone down and warmed her. The air around her was like a song, filled with the melodies of hundreds of twittering, trilling, ecstatic birds. Fresh, shining, green leaves on hundreds of trees swished and whispered all around her.

The feeling that everything had happened the way it did for a reason washed over Sam suddenly—like every action she'd taken and every decision she'd made all fit together like a jigsaw puzzle, even though she hadn't known it. But was she a piece of the puzzle, or the one putting it together? *Maybe both*, she thought.

She felt peaceful by the time they reached Birchwood. Sam was exhausted, but she knew for sure this was the right thing to do, no matter how much trouble she was in. No matter how much she'd miss Horatio.

Now that he was finally here, Horatio stopped trying to tug away from Sam. He pressed close to her and looked around, panting hard.

"Hello, Sam!" said the receptionist. "You certainly are here early. Hey—that's not Piglet! Who have you got there?"

"This is Horatio. He's going to be the new resident therapy dog here. Mrs. Goodard and I talked about it." Suddenly Sam was afraid that now that she was finally here, somebody would stop her from bringing Horatio in. "Is she here yet?"

"She is. I'll just call her," said the receptionist, picking up the phone.

Mrs. Goodard appeared in a billow of perfume.

"There you are, Sam! And this is the amazing Horatio?"

"Yes, this is the dog."

Mrs. Goodard bent to pat him, and the shaggy dog lolloped over to her and leaned in. He pushed his head into her hand, snuggling into the attention.

"What a friendly dog! Well if he's like this all the time, he'll make a perfect resident dog. Shall we go to the common room and let everyone meet him?"

"Yes," said Sam, praying that Mrs. Sylvan was in her room and not in the common room. She hadn't forgotten that residents weren't allowed to bring their own pets to Birchwood. The home could accommodate one shared dog, but if all the residents tried to bring their own pets, it would be too crowded. The reunion between Stella and her dog might give the whole game away. Sam hoped she hadn't come this far just to have her entire plan fail.

The common room was as bright and noisy as usual. Sam waved to everyone.

"That's not Piglet!" several of them shouted.

"Bring your new dog over here!" somebody called.

"Oh, what a gorgeous big dog!" said another.

Soon the room was quiet while everyone admired Horatio. He was in his glory. Far from being intimidated by so many strangers in a new setting, he moved from person to person, radiating and receiving love like a Tibetan lama. The quiet feeling she'd had earlier that morning filled Sam again. She unclipped Horatio's leash and watched him fill the room with peace.

In a flash, Sam realized she wasn't completely losing him. Even though he would never be her dog, her *own* dog, she'd be able to see him when she came to Birchwood. Twice a week!

Mrs. Goodard observed the dog and the residents. Sam waited, sure of what the director's decision would be. Finally Mrs. Goodard said, "Well, Sam, I must thank you. You've brought the perfect dog here to Birchwood. I couldn't have dreamt of any dog better suited to this place. We'll definitely give him a home."

"Oh, thank you! You won't regret it. He's going to make everyone here so happy," said Sam.

"I think he already has." Mrs. Goodard pointed at all the smiling faces in the room. Then she said, "I need to do a few things. You're okay here, aren't you? Let me know when you go. I'll take Horatio from you."

She was gone. Sam took a deep breath and turned to go to Mrs. Sylvan's room. She had only gone a few steps when she heard a voice that stopped her instantly.

"Samantha Hudson!" It was Mom. What was she doing here? She was going to ruin everything!

Sam turned around then jerked sideways as Horatio kept pulling her down the hall. Had he smelled Stella already?

"What on earth is going on? How dare you disappear like that? Don't you know how worried I was about you? I was about to call the police. Luckily Jasmeet knew you intended to bring Horatio to Birchwood this morning, so I came here first."

Horatio tugged, but Sam stood absolutely still, trying to figure out if Mom was going to hug her or haul her out to the car. Mom seemed to be trying to figure it out too. She regarded Sam with an unwavering stony stare.

"Mom," Sam finally said, "I told you I promised Mrs. Goodard to bring Horatio here. You knew how worried I was about him. I had to do it."

Mom folded her arms over her chest. "You *had* to sneak out of the house? I can't believe…"

"Mom, listen to me. There's more—something really amazing."

Mom cocked her head and raised her eyebrows. Before she could object, Horatio gave a great heave and pulled Sam down the hall a few steps.

"Sam—"

"Just come with me, Mom. I have to do something important. Then I'll come home with you and you can ground me for life."

Then Horatio was bounding down the hall, dragging Sam behind him. She didn't even look to see whether Mom was following.

. . .

STELLA AND SAM

The big black dog hurled himself into the small room, seeming to fill it up. He began keening, singing out to Stella. He ran to her, whirling and bouncing.

Stella watched her dog dance in front of her. Here he was—just the way she had imagined him so many times! It was a miracle.

"Luh Buh!" she shouted at the top of her lungs.

The dog boomed a deep woof from the depths of his chest. He put his paws on the armrests of Stella's wheelchair and licked her face, his tail lashing faster than Sam had ever seen it.

Stella could feel the warmth and wetness of her dog's kisses. It seemed like the first thing she'd been able to feel since her stroke. She lifted her hands carefully, heavily, to pat him and gasped as her skin remembered the soft silkiness of his fur.

Sam watched them, wishing only that she had figured out the connection sooner. They deserved to be together. She glanced back at Mom, silent and still in the doorway. The reunion between the bouncing dog and smiling woman in the wheelchair was worth it, no matter what happened next.

Stella looked at Sam, who had taken such good care of the dog. He was as healthy and happy as she had ever seen him. "Tak yuh," she said.

"You're welcome," said Sam to Stella.

"Okay, we can go now," she said to her mother.

Chapter 16

SAM

WHEN THE HEAVY DOORS TO BIRCHWOOD swung shut behind her, Sam's feeling of peace was gone, like a bubble popping. Now she felt like her head was holding up a hatful of rocks.

They were silent in the car. The world still looked as beautiful to Sam as it had earlier. It was as though she could see each leaf all by itself, and the whole world shining in it. But she couldn't enjoy it, knowing how much trouble she would be in once they got home.

"Sam, how could you do this to me? Sneaking out of the house without telling me? Climbing down the fire-escape ladder? You have no idea how worried I was," said Mom once they were inside, sitting at the kitchen table. "You put yourself in such danger." She twisted her hands together.

"I had to, Mom."

"I can't believe you would do something like this." Mom looked at Sam and shook her head, like she was trying to see more clearly. "Why didn't you just *tell* me about all of this in the first place?"

"Because you never listen to me. You don't hear what I really say."

"Oh, Sam..."

"Sometimes I know what's important and what I need to do," Sam couldn't stop herself from saying. She tried to sound responsible and mature. "And when I do, I decide to make it happen, no matter what. No matter how hard it seems or whether you don't want me to. But you could never believe that. I didn't know why I was doing what I did with Horatio, but now I know I was right. Look at how it turned out. Imagine how worried Stella must have been—how much she must have missed Horatio."

"You're right, Sam, and that was a good thing you did. But don't you ever, ever do anything like that again. You tell me when you have a problem, don't sneak around behind my back and..."

"If I had told you about Horatio when I found him you would have taken him to the pound and Stella wouldn't have got her dog back."

"Sam!" Mom spat out the word sharply.

Sam hung her head. She had gone too far. Now here it came, the big trouble. Nothing she could do about it. But Mom was silent for a long time.

"Sam, if I promise to listen better," she finally said in a gentle voice, "and pay attention to what you say, will you promise to tell me the next time you come up with a crazy scheme like this?"

Sam could hardly believe what she was hearing. Mom had never offered Sam this kind of deal. What was the catch? Sam peeked up at Mom, but Mom looked limp, her arms hanging down beside her, like she was out of batteries. Mom meant it.

"Okay, I promise," said Sam.

Amazingly, Mom smiled. Then she continued, "I can see that you handled a difficult situation as well as you could. Will you tell me how you took care of Horatio? How on earth did you ever get that huge bag of dog food home?"

Mom's voice was so gentle, so unlike her usual self that Sam decided to tell her everything.

"I'm impressed," Mom said when Sam was finished. "You lied and sneaked around, but you did take good care of Horatio. I'm proud to see you becoming a more responsible person. I'm still angry with you for being dishonest, but maybe the end does justify the means in this case."

Sam didn't move. It *couldn't* be possible that she wasn't in trouble.

"Sam, I see how well you're growing up. I'm sorry I didn't see it sooner. You're going to be twelve soon, and I guess that's old enough to take charge of some things for yourself."

Sam took a deep breath and dared to ask, "Mom, would you listen to me if I said I didn't want to keep taking soccer and piano lessons?"

Mom shook her head, smiling. "You really are growing up. Let's talk about it later." Then she added, "You must have gotten up pretty early this morning to go out and get Horatio. Go take a bath, and I'll bring you up a cup of hot cocoa."

"Thanks," said Sam, hardly daring to believe that it was all over. Mom hadn't found out she'd been out all night!

It *was* over. Sam was free.

She gave Mom a big bear hug. Mom hugged her back, and Sam felt an unexpected warmth: she melted into the hug, the way she had with Horatio. It was different.

Maybe everything would be different now.

. . .

STELLA

Stella was watching the birds again. Spring was filling the world, and the berries and bugs out in the wide world were becoming more and more plentiful, so the birds at the feeder outside Stella's window were becoming fewer and fewer. Soon they would be gone for the summer, off hatching and feeding and raising and teaching their baby birds. But the baby birds would join them at the feeder next winter. Stella knew this would happen. She had seen it before, year after year.

The approaching absence of the birds didn't bother her, not today. Today Little Bear was here, stretched out at her feet, getting as close to her as the wheelchair allowed. He licked her hand, blinked his eyes at her, twitched his ears, walked across the room and lay in the doorway, guarding the entrance to Stella's room.

She smiled. In between his rounds, when he visited every dog lover at Birchwood, Horatio came back to Stella's room to rest and relax. Now she was never alone.

The dog could not remember ever being happier. He was finally living back at home with her again, and she gave him chicken every night for dinner. Better still, each morning he did the very important job of visiting all his new friends at the big place. He knew he needed to bounce into their days, making them special and bright. It was the best job he ever could have imagined, because he got all the love and pats and biscuits he wanted. He stayed with each person until they didn't need him any more, and then he visited the next. And every night he was with her, the one who needed him most of all.

Plus, the girl came every day after school to walk with him. They went on longer walks together than ever before, and she didn't seem worried anymore, which was good. He, too, could relax and play on the walks, sniffing for fun instead of trying to track down the most important person in his world.

Because she was with him all the time.

MICHELLE SUPERLE loves all dogs, especially big
ones. When she's not out playing with dogs or
writing books, she teaches writing courses at
Okanagan College in Kelowna, BC. This is her
first published novel for young people.

MILLIE BALLANCE lived in Vancouver for many
years before moving back to her native England.
She also illustrated the award-winning *Eco Diary
of Kiran Singer* for Tradewind Books.